SNIPER

ALSO BY THEODORE TAYLOR

The Cay
Teetoncey
Teetoncey and Ben O'Neal
The Odyssey of Ben O'Neal
The Trouble with Tuck
The Maldonado Miracle
Sweet Friday Island
Walking Up a Rainbow
The Hostage

The Cats of Shambala (with Tippi Hedren)

SNIPER

THEODORE TAYLOR

HARCOURT BRACE JOVANOVICH
PUBLISHERS
SAN DIEGO NEW YORK LONDON

Copyright © 1989 by Theodore Taylor

Requests for permission to make copies of any
part of the work should be mailed to:
Permissions Department,
Harcourt Brace Jovanovich, Publishers, 8th Floor,
Orlando, Florida 32887.

"Mammas Don't Let Your Babies Grow Up to Be Cowboys"
by Ed Bruce, Patsy Bruce, copyright © 1975 Tree Publishing Co.,
Inc. All rights reserved. International copyright secured. Used by
permission of the publisher.

Library of Congress Cataloging-in-Publication Data
Taylor, Theodore, 1922–
Sniper/Theodore Taylor. — 1st ed.
p. cm.
Summary: Fifteen-year-old Ben must cope alone when a
mysterious sniper begins shooting the big cats in his family's
private zoological preserve.
ISBN 0-15-276420-8
[1. Cats — Fiction.   2. Felidae — Fiction.   3. Zoos — Fiction.]
1. Title.
PZ7.T2186n   1989
[Fic] — dcl9   89-7415

Design by Dalia Hartman

Printed in the United States of America

D E F G

For Tippi Hedren
with Love

SNIPER

When Ben met his first fully grown lion, his dad said, "Wait and maybe he'll come up to you. Just stand still. He might brush up against you, or maybe he'll stop and take your shoulder into his mouth. Don't resist it, don't be scared. You've seen a lot of big cats from a distance."

On he came, almost five hundred pounds, with a massive brown-black mane, huge eyes targeted on the boy. His name was Reggie, and he'd grown up in captivity, though he was never a circus or zoo cat. He made movies and TV commercials.

Eight at the time, Ben was truly frightened, though his dad was only a few feet away. But he had no gun, no weapon of any kind. His dad didn't believe in guns. The nearest thing to a weapon he had ever used was a fire extinguisher, a whoosh in the face of a big cat.

"Don't turn your back on him. He has a sense of humor, likes to come up behind people and trip them. So if you run or make fast movements, he'll think you want to play, and he plays rough. If you want to pet him, use strong, firm scratching. Otherwise, it's like a fly getting at him. Scratch under his chin or deep into the mane but not on his face. He's very dignified."

By then, Reggie was no more than two feet away, and Ben saw the big mouth open wide, felt the hot breath; then the canines, looking like ivory daggers, grasped his shoulder.

Ben closed his eyes as the teeth held him.

"You see, you've made a friend," said his dad, laughing softly.

Ben stood absolutely still, hardly breathing, momentarily paralyzed, then felt the pressure on his shoulder being removed.

As he opened his eyes, Reggie was walking majestically away, tail knot swinging like a pendulum, and Ben would never forget the relief he felt; at the same instant, the thrill of finally having met the king of beasts face-to-face.

"But, believe me, Ben, not all lions are like Reggie. We'll probably have some here that won't be friendly at all."

FIRST DAY

Los Coyotes Preserve

As if jabbed with a long needle, Benjamin Jepson jerked awake to screams of peacocks. Heart slamming for a few seconds, he sat bolt upright, looking outside toward the abrasive, metallic sounds.

Who's out there? What's bothering them? he thought as the high-pitched screaming continued.

Trying to collect his senses, Ben scrambled out of bed, remembering his dad's warning never to turn on room lights when alarms rang. Any alarms, including the stupid peacocks. Night vision might well be needed out in those deep shadows around the trees and bushes and in the sandy paths along the animal compounds.

His dad, Dr. Peter Jepson, was director of Los Coyotes Preserve, their private zoological resource specializing in big cat study. They had both the *Panthera*, large roaring cats such as lions and tigers, and the *Felis*, smaller purring cats such as cougars.

"Ben, you just never know what the danger may be

till you're facing it. Sometimes that's too close, much too close."

Always sleeping naked, winter or summer, Ben groped around for his clothes—worn Levi's and a wash-whitened denim shirt; cowboy-style boots, scuffed and dusty; his Zacatecas straw hat, one like Willie Nelson sometimes wore, treasured gift of chief handler Alfredo Garcia. Straw hat over straw hair, shading an ordinary freckled face, the feather-banded hat was as much a part of Ben as the dusty boots. He wore it constantly.

The din kept up, and he could feel the presence of Rachel, their large house cheetah, but couldn't see her. Just the same, he was certain that she was sitting up, also hearing the raucous shrilling, amber eyes searching the darkness.

Four of the gaudy birds paraded around outside during the day, common males with long green and gold erectile tails. None too bright, frequently noisy and aggressive, they rested peacefully most nights in the lower branches of the tall cottonwoods.

The silly peacocks were sometimes the best alarm, witless as they were about most other things. Often better than the electronic system on the two main gates, or the sensitized, barbed strand at the top of the perimeter fencing.

They were certainly better alerts than any of the unreliable compound animals. When intruders came around, the sly, suspicious tigers usually stayed dead silent, waiting in the murk for a victim. So did the leopards and jaguars. But the more excitable lions would sometimes roar at nocturnal invasions of either humans or hapless small animals.

Sometimes crazies, total wackos, total loonies, traveling along the lonely Orange County road, would decide to pay a visit, climb the fourteen-foot-high chain-link perimeter fence, then scale the individual compound fences to drop down into the cat pens like fat geese, playing with death.

Wackos! Loonies!

Two years ago, a drug-blitzed girl of fifteen had jumped down on two lionesses on an incredibly dumb dare. Sobering up instantly, she climbed an oak. Ben's mother, a light sleeper, heard the screams. Had the pink-haired girl chosen the next compound over, Dmitri, the huge Siberian tiger, would have been waiting.

Good-bye, punk rocker from El Toro.

Another stupid, wacko crazy out there, Ben thought, wide awake now and angry at the intruder, pulling up his pants, letting his shirt fall free. He didn't need a jacket. June in the southern California back country was always warm enough for shirt sleeves, even at night.

Just what made people do it? Some insane challenge to the cats? He couldn't imagine any more painful, traumatic way to die. Lacerated by three-inch teeth. Eaten alive. The cats didn't know any better. They were absolutely innocent. Meat was meat, animal or human, and there was no remorse, his father said.

Ben saw a shadowy Rachel go over to the window, looking out.

"Who's there, Rachel?" he asked, hooking his belt, hearing his own voice wound up tight, feeling a ticking in his throat, speeding of pulse, dryness of mouth.

He glanced over at the blue face of the nearby clock. Four-fifteen, Tuesday morning. Ten days since they had gone.

He now wished they, illustrious globe-hopping father and mother, were home in Los Coyotes, especially his dad. He didn't take guff from anyone, wackos or not. Neither did his mother, in fact. But it was a totally useless wish. They were in Africa, somewhere deep in the Serengeti, that vast wildlife park in Tanzania, doing a magazine piece on poaching.

They'd left Alfredo Garcia to run the preserve. But two days ago a truck crashed head-on into Alfredo's old Buick on El Toro Road, and the chunky Latino was now in intensive care, expected to live but badly injured. Fractured skull, left leg broken, some internal injuries.

Like it or not, Ben Jepson was suddenly in charge of Los Coyotes. In three weeks he'd be fifteen.

There had been only a small piece of fading moon earlier that night when Ben had walked the pathways along the compounds with his girlfriend, Sandy Gilmore. Now it was black as the inside of a burial vault out there. Darker the night, quieter the animals, always. Spooky, sometimes.

The cats didn't need light, and bright illumination only drew road attention to the preserve. Besides, it was too expensive, his dad said. But Ben at this moment was wishing, also useless, that the place could be lit up like a baseball park, erasing all shadows. Out there were shadows upon shadows, all in evil shapes, threatening webs and patches and blurs.

Pulling his boots on, Ben realized he was delaying going out. *I should be moving faster!* No guts.

"Why did it have to happen now?" he said to Rachel. "Why? And why did Alfredo have to wreck?"

The last crazy had been more than a year ago. Cackling, nutty old man cut a hole through the perimeter fence, then through a compound fence. A cub was what he was after, he told Deputy Sheriff Metcalf.

There were no cubs at Los Coyotes at that time.

"Certain screwy people are capable of almost anything," said Deputy Metcalf.

Maybe a human crazy wasn't out there, after all. Maybe it was just a brave raccoon snooping around the aviary? That had happened, too. Everyone relaxed and laughed.

Ah, *mapache*. Sneaky raccoon.

Telling Rachel to stay put, he went through the bedroom doorway, on through the dining space, out through the living room, stopping for a second by the front door to reach down for the long-barreled twenty-thousand-candlepower flashlight. They always carried it when going out into the night, both for illumination and as a weapon against human prowlers. It would be useless as a feather against an already charging cat.

The peacocks were still screeching from their roosts when Ben got outside, obviously scared silly over some alien presence. But, oddly enough, not one of the big cats was roaring. Not even the lions. That in itself was ominous to Ben. Did they know something?

Shining the light toward the aviary, to the left of their old three-bedroom house, Ben's boots were almost soundless in the loose, soft sand of the preserve roadway. It was indeed velvet black out there at twenty-five after four, making the beam precise and brilliant.

There was movement off to the right, barely perceptible, and he swung the torch over there, gasping as he picked up two large, round, coppery green eyes in the glow; then the tawny body of a big cat, frozen in the brilliance of the beam.

He stopped dead still. Frozen, too.

No drug-blitzed rocker staggering around this warm June night. No *mapache!*

"God," he said, reverently, almost in a whisper.

He was in absolute awe.

"God, they're out!"

Nothing more chilling could be said around any preserve or zoo.

From sixty feet that one looked like Missy, a middle-aged, mellow cat. She lived in Number Three compound with Daisy and Helen. Yes, it was Missy, he was certain. All three were mostly mellow. But where were the other two? He knew them by their distinctive faces. They knew him by voice and sight.

Gentle, motherly Helen and aging Daisy were among his favorites. They were animals you could hug, put your cheek against their warm necks, see the affection in their eyes when you paid attention to them. Around the preserve they were called "The Sisters," always grooming each other.

"It's me—Ben," he said loudly, knowing Missy was blinded by the intense light.

First-name basis to a lioness might sound silly, if not downright ridiculous, but to stay alive and healthy in Los Coyotes a close family-type relationship was absolutely necessary. Friends! Good friends. Nice kitty with the big teeth.

Shooting the light over to Number Three, Ben saw that the gate stood half open. No animals inside. Next he moved the powerful beam to Number Two, some ninety feet away. Three lions usually lived there. One of them was his own Rocky, always sweet and loving to him but treacherous nowadays with other people.

Where was Rocky?

Number Two was also half open. They'd never bothered to use padlocks.

Who'd done this? And why?

There were twenty-eight compounds, one to four acres each, each holding up to eight cats. Up in Number One was Dmitri, a loner, and if he was out, Ben knew exactly what he was going to do: go hellbent for the house, get inside, lock the door, and wait for dawn.

Though his mother had bottle-nursed Dimmy as a cub, fully grown the Siberian tiger was terrifying. Thirteen sleek, gorgeous feet from the tip of his tail to the tip of his wide nose, he weighed seven hundred and thirty pounds. He'd scalped her once when he was three, laying the bloody mat of hair and skin over her forehead. He was six now, set in his ways, a hermit.

Throat dry, mouth parched with sudden fear because of the Siberian, heart slamming again, Ben moved slowly ahead until he could see the tiger's compound.

Dimmy was always fed on the end of a shovel, red muscle meat and innards inserted through a six-by-ten-inch slot in the bottom of the fence. When he was moved to another compound, a welcome change of scenery in the usual rotation of living quarters, it was inside a squeeze cage with one-inch steel bars.

Despite his ferocity, or perhaps because of it, Dmitri was a favorite of Ben's father. He alone could go in with

Dmitri, hugging him, rubbing his neck. The great Siberian would moan with pleasure. But only Peter Jepson could do that and live to walk out.

Ben stopped by the gate of Number Two compound, shining the light over toward the tiger's residence, knowing he could jump inside Number Two, bang the gate shut if Dimmy was loose; stay there until daylight and hope the tiger wouldn't take his wrath out on the lions. But there he was, striped head staring curiously from his hut, greenish eyes impaled by the beam.

"Thank God."

Whoever had released the other cats had enough good sense not to unleash Dmitri.

Ben let out a long sigh of relief and ran in the opposite direction, toward the trailers where the two other Latino handlers lived.

Oh, did he need Alfredo at this moment! He needed his calm strength, needed his know-how.

Knocking on the handlers' door, Ben spoke rapidly in Spanish, *"¡Gata fuera! ¡Gata fuera!"* Cat out! Even groggy with sleep, Luis Vargas and Rafael Soto didn't need to hear anything else. They were up instantly.

Ben spoke some limited Spanish, having learned from Alfredo. He added needlessly, *"Andale! Andale!"* Hurry! Hurry!

Thinking about Rocky, he ran back toward the aviary, where the peacocks were still caterwauling in the trees.

Shots in the Night

Luis and Rafael stumbled into the darkness carrying flashlights and half-inch chain leads with steel rings on either end, one large, one small. As they ran up the pathway to the forward part of the preserve, joining Ben in the search, Luis quickly asked if he knew which cats were loose. Wiry, hard-muscled, mustachioed little Luis Vargas spoke English, having been raised in New Mexico, though born below the border.

Spreading out, they moved slowly, cautiously, through the brush, now and then catching glints of liquid green in the beams.

Ben said, "Dmitri is still in his compound."

"*Muy bueno,*" said Rafael Soto, *very good*, grunting a nervous laugh as Luis translated. Soto spoke no English.

Yes, it was very good that the vicious Siberian was still in his space, behind steel.

"But Rocky's out," Ben warned.

"Oh, oh, *muy malo*," said Soto, *very bad*, as Luis translated again.

"*Sí,*" said Ben, *yes, you're right.*

The frightening thing at night was lack of immediate identification. Did those coppery eyes belong to Helen or Daisy? They would come along without resistance. Or did they belong to Rocky, who might charge if someone was with Ben?

Rocky: Ben's self-appointed protector, very much a one-man cat. Ben had raised him from infancy, a rejected cub.

"Talk as you walk," he told the Latinos. He wanted the cats to hear familiar voices.

They began to jabber.

Then, just ahead and off to the left, was Rocky, un-mistakable, big-eyed head and licorice-black spikes of mane visible in the ivory circle of light. He was staring toward the advancing humans but didn't seem poised to charge. He was just standing there, puzzled.

"Luis, come over on the right side of me and drop back," Ben said, trying to hide the uneasiness in his voice.

"Drop back, Rafael."

Luis and Rafael were relatively inexperienced and knew little about big cat mentality. The lights were con-fusing and blinding Rocky, but his hearing was finely tuned and accurate. He could hear leaves fall, the beat of hum-mingbird wings, a feather hitting the ground.

Rocky knew they were approaching.

"Good boy, Rocky, just stay right there. Ben's here!"

The lion roared suddenly, shifting his weight, moving back and forth on his front paws nervously, rocking his huge body, obviously trying to decide whether or not to charge at Rafael and Luis. He flicked his tail up in the air, an early warning sign. If it went horizontal, he'd already be charging.

"Be a good boy, Rocky," Ben repeated, pleading this time. "Good boy."

Luis crooned, *"Tranquilamente*, Rocky," dropping back.

Rocky's roaring was picked up in the farthest compounds and began to travel eerily, fenced area by fenced area. Most times the roaring of the cats was pleasing, but this charcoal morning it was unnerving. It echoed up the canyon, becoming menacing. The leopards added to the noise with their guttural barks, the jaguars with their coughing roars—five or six notes—the cougars with whistling sounds. And the peacocks had begun screeching again.

Cacophony.

With Rafael behind him, Ben got to within six feet of his lion, ready to throw a lead around his neck. But Rocky broke to the right, galloping up the roadway.

Ben said, "Okay, let him go. Let's get the others." They were less dangerous animals in this situation.

He walked right up to Missy, tossing the lead around her neck, and she was soon back in her space, flopping down as if nothing had happened.

But Helen, Daisy, and the three males, Rocky, Chico and Mikey, remained loose somewhere in the darkness.

The individual compounds were opposite each other at a distance of about four hundred feet. Between them was an area of vines, bushes, grass, and trees; some flower beds. The Rio Naranja was broken into meandering streams so that each compound was watered by a tiny branch of the river. Surrounded on three sides by big cat residences, the Jepsons' pleasant old board-and-batten house was near the aviary and those upper compounds that had been opened

13

by someone, maybe some crazy, this tar-colored morning.

The missing cats had obviously gone north, and Ben thought they were likely still within the perimeter fencing. The greatest danger was that they might try to dig out. The compound fencing had four feet of concrete footing, resistant to the sharpest claws. But the perimeter fencing penetrated into the sand no more than six inches, something they'd been planning to take care of for months.

Ben said to Luis, "Tell Rafael to wake up Dr. Odinga and have him bring a dart gun."

The darts, loaded with phencyclidine and atropine, were always used as a last resort to sedate the cats. Dosage was critical, and the animals had to be hit in the flanks. There were plenty of known cases where cats had died after taking hits in the stomach. Using a dart on Rocky would be a last resort.

Rafael loped away.

Hudson Odinga

Hudson Odinga was a string-bean Kenyan with a craggy, shining face that looked as if it had been carved out of anthracite. He was a Kikuyu, born on a Dutchman's farm in the white highlands of Kenya, goatherd until he was fifteen, when he joined the Mau Mau in 1954.

Ben's dad said Hudson had done his share of killing white farmers on raiding parties out of the Aberdare. Ben was impressed but also leery of the black man.

Odinga was waiting to take his National Boards and the state veterinary exams, having been at the preserve three months. For lack of a better title, he was their temporary resident vet. Ben's dad provided shelter and a little money while Hudson studied. The health of the big cats was basically good, and he usually had little to do except repair minor fight wounds and spray antibiotics on them. His vet papers from Nairobi were legitimate but essentially useless in California.

While they waited near the gate to compound Number Three, Ben asked Luis, "Who could have done this?"

"I do not know. Those gates were closed after feeding yesterday, I tell you. I'm sure of that. We did not go out last night." He was talking about himself and Rafael. "I do not know about the African."

That was Hudson, of course. He didn't have a car, so it wasn't likely he was the gate culprit, accidentally or not. The strict orders were: *Make sure the gates are closed.* In or out. Around the clock.

Ben said, "Well, someone came in through one of them, and the bell didn't ring."

There was a loud bell for the gates centrally located in the kitchen. The system was automatically activated by nightfall.

"Or someone came over the outside fencing," Luis ventured.

Ben could barely see the swarthy, angular face. Just the harsh whites of his eyes. "The perimeter alarm didn't ring."

Luis said, "We were asleep, Ben," as if he and Rafael were being accused of negligence.

"I'm sure you were. I'm not blaming you, Luis. I don't know who's to blame."

In the six years that the preserve had been down in the canyon, cats had been out only a few times, and then only by accident. Carelessness while the spaces were being cleaned of dung, fresh straw being put down in the huts. Or while the cats were being rotated, the biweekly procedure established by Ben's dad so they'd have new things to look at, new trees to claw. Rotation prevented boredom and pacing.

Ben said, "Well, I'm buying padlocks tomorrow for every single compound. You take one set of keys. I'll take the other. We should have done it before."

Take charge, he said to himself. *Do it now!* Locking the compound gates had never been considered necessary, but times were changing. More crazies moving around the county.

Luis said, "Okay, Ben," looking at the boy strangely. Boss, now, eh?

"After daylight take a check on the gate security system and see if the wiring on the perimeter fence is all right."

Ben was desperately trying to echo his dad or Alfredo, think like they might think, act like they might act. He was "Ben-hamin," son of Pedro, the director. Much was expected of him.

Luis said he'd make the check.

They waited, looking at the shadows ahead, listening. Not much was stealthier than a cat, big or little, loose in the night.

Then Rafael and Hudson Odinga came up, the latter holding the tranquilizer pistol, a Luger type.

Again worried about aiming in the torch glow, Ben said to Odinga, "Don't shoot unless he looks like he's going to charge."

Give orders, he said to himself. *Say them firmly.*

Not looking like anyone who would kill white farmers, the tall, dignified Kenyan, who often wore a coat and tie, even to study, nodded, and off they went again, spread about six feet apart now, heading toward the northern end of the preserve, up through that four-hundred-foot strip of brush and trees that separated the two rows of compounds.

"Keep talking," Ben reminded. About anything.

He wasn't worried about the lions rushing without warning and didn't intend to get them cornered. By now, with all the lights and voices, the cats probably just wanted to return home to safety.

Ben said, "No kid came in and did this."

The British-tanged "Darth Vader" voice of Hudson Odinga came out of the darkness, off to the right. "Who are your enemies?" he asked.

Before Ben could answer, green glints were picked up over toward Number Six compound. Then a big beige body formed behind the glistening eyes.

"That's Chico, my old friend." Luis laughed.

"*A todos nos gusta alguna vez echar cana al aire*," he said to the lion. *We all like to go on a spree once in a while.*

Luis laughed heartily, peeling off to go drape a lead around Chico's neck, starting him back to Number Two. Chico was almost fifteen years old, usually harmless.

A few hundred feet further, playful young Mikey was spotted, ambling toward the lake.

Rafael Soto went over, leashed him without a problem, and also headed for Number Two.

That left The Sisters, Helen and Daisy, and Rocky lion hiding someplace.

Ben kept walking slowly, Hudson by his side, light shining back and forth, probing the knee-high grass around the bases of the cottonwoods and oaks, poking into the higher bushes.

They did have enemies. Some neighbors stayed annoyed just because the cats were there. His dad said that was understandable.

Ben said to Hudson, "The old people, the Carpenters, in the trailer park down the road, they're always afraid the cats'll get out. Some of the ranchers, like Mrs. Mesko, next door, are afraid of horse or cattle attack. She's got prize horses. Then we've got some real oddballs back in here.

Hunter types. Rednecks. But we've seldom had problems."
Only two serious cases: one with the Carpenters, the other
with the Meskos. Cat invasions.

"What are rednecks?" the Kenyan asked.

Ben had to think. "They talk loud and shoot little animals like squirrels just for fun. They drink a lot." He knew
the description wasn't adequate.

"Rednecks," Hudson repeated. "I think I know what
you mean."

"They're everywhere, I'd bet, even in Kenya," Ben
said, his light catching an eye glint to their left in shoulder-
high bushes. "They . . ." Ben stopped talking and in a
whisper said to Odinga, "I think that's Rocky. Get out of
sight . . ."

Ben stood still a moment, keeping the beam on the
eye glint and the shadowy form of the lion, then said in a
friendly voice while slowly walking toward the bushes,
"Hey, Rock, what the devil you doin' out this time o'
night . . ." There'd been playtimes a while back when Rocky
hid in these same bushes. But this wasn't playtime.

The lion didn't move, and Ben said, "Remember this
game." That was four years ago when Rocky was a big,
rowdy cub.

Pushing aside the bushes with his right hand, Ben said,
"Who let you out, huh?" dropping the lead in his left hand
around Rocky's neck.

Then he stood by the lion another few minutes,
scratching deep into his mane. "Everything's okay, Rock.
We'll be going back home in a minute."

Finally, Ben led Rocky back to Number Two, knowing
he'd passed a silent Hudson Odinga who wisely stood waiting in the darkness.

Ten minutes later, they were searching for Helen and

Daisy just to the north of where Ben had spotted Rocky.

"You have any problems with him?" Odinga asked.

"No, I never do when I'm by myself. He's been single-minded jealous for almost six months now. Something popped in his head. It came on suddenly, and I don't . . ."

Ben stopped, holding his light on a hump of yellow-brown over in the high grass.

He began running over there, Odinga following. "It's Helen. She's down . . ."

Helen lay still, open eyes glazed. Blood leaked from her mouth, staining her canines, turning the grass a deep crimson. In the harsh glow of the torch, there appeared to be a grimace on her face, as if she'd sniffed someone.

"She's dead, Hudson," Ben said, looking up unbelievingly. "She's dead."

Dr. Odinga knelt down and felt Helen's heart, holding his hand on the breast of the lioness. "Yes, she's dead, Benjamin." He felt around, and his hand came up red. "Gunshot, I believe."

Then Ben saw, dimly, another hump of yellow and brown and ran over to it.

Daisy! Seventeen-year-old Daisy.

"Hudson," he called out, and the Kenyan came over to stand beside Ben, looking down.

The beam of light revealed the lioness in her death throe, blood from the mouth, brown eyes open and glazed.

Ben was stunned as well as frightened. The Sisters were dead! Why Helen? Why Daisy? They were kind, gentle cats.

"Who did this awful thing?" he asked, tears welling.

A half hour later, as dawn oranges and yellows began to emerge over the low chaparral mountains to the east, Ben sat on the dew-wet redwood plank porch, vacantly staring, eyes smarting, first up toward the road, then off toward the compounds. He was still in shock and feeling totally alone.

Ten or twenty lions were roaring in sequence, as if cued, starting at the far end of the preserve, but he scarcely heard them. There was the usual early morning racket from the duck pond, the mallards and pintails squabbling as thin fog rose from the still water. They, too, went unheard by Ben. The green oasis-like beauty of the canyon, always so fresh at daybreak, winter or summer, went unseen.

Sitting there, he still couldn't believe that Helen and Daisy were gone forever, killed by terrible bullets. For the first time in his life he also wanted to kill. This time a different kind of crazy might be prowling the compounds. Feeling drained inside, he got up from the porch to dig a deep hole with the backhoe and bury the lionesses, both rage and sorrow burning within him.

Guiding the noisy secondhand machine, steel bucket eating into sandy soil, Helen and Daisy wrapped in green tarps a few feet away, Ben found himself fighting tears again, jaw quivering.

They'd had animals die from time to time, cubs especially, and he'd felt sorrow for them but never like this. He'd lost close friends this morning. Their deaths made no sense, and what he really wanted to do was cry an ocean, but he held it back because Hudson was standing there.

At his grandfather's funeral, Ben had noticed tears

rolling down his dad's face. Yet his mother stood expressionless. But it was her father, *her own father*, who had died. He didn't understand.

That night, his mother in another room, Ben asked his dad about it. "Your mother loved him very much," he replied, "but she keeps her grief inside—bottles it up."

"And you don't?"

"Obviously, I don't. I can't."

"Have you ever seen Mother cry?"

"No."

Ben had thought about that from time to time, her never crying. It was true, he realized. She never did cry. Whenever they watched a sad movie together, Ben would hear his dad sniffling. Then he'd look over, and his mother would be sitting there dry-eyed.

Now, one part of him said, *Cry an ocean*; another part said, *Act like a man*.

Maybe somewhere in the middle was how it should be.

But one thing he knew for certain was that he didn't want to keep grief bottled up like his mother. His dad said it wasn't healthy, and Ben knew he was right.

The hole was now about seven feet deep, with a width of five, enough for Helen's grave. The earth was turning gray at that depth, getting damp, though they were well away from the lake and the Naranja, out by a blue oak. Next he dug a grave for Daisy.

Parking the backhoe, clenching his teeth, he said, "Okay, let's do it," and Hudson grabbed one end of the tarp. Ben took the other, and they slid Helen into the hole, then the same for Daisy.

Ben could barely say, "You cover them," as he headed off toward the house, walking on leaden legs.

Was it the same person who'd opened the compound gates? Had he intended to let all the animals out? The questions kept bouncing around in Ben's head. Crazies again? Rednecks who had something against fenced animals?

In past twilights out on the porch, Ben's parents had argued between themselves and also with visiting zoologists about the rights and wrongs of keeping captive animals. His mother always felt some guilt about big cats behind fences. "Nature didn't intend them to be prisoners," she claimed.

Ben leaned toward his mother on that one.

"Dot, they live longer here," argued his dad. "Their lives are easier. They don't have to go out and hunt food. They get the best of medical care."

"But the quality of the shorter life in freedom might be far better than existence behind chain-link," she said.

His dad countered that they helped the lions and lionesses do what they did best—be lazy.

As Ben had grown older, he was for the "shorter life" and freedom, but his father told stories of savanna lions starving to death because of a jaw injury, of cubs being abandoned, of the deadly steel snares and bullets of poachers, of thousands of animals dying because of a simple blood parasite, easily curable in captivity.

The answer wasn't simple.

All the Los Coyotes cats had been bred in captivity and would die in captivity. None could be returned to the wild, anyway, because they could never cope for themselves. The old truth.

"At least our animals are safe and sound here," his dad had said. Well, not anymore.

Dorothy Courtney-Jepson

Sandy Gilmore had said, "You're glad they're going." Father and mother up, up and away in the big metal bird. "Aren't you? I can tell."

Yep. Glad.

She said, "We'll have you over to dinner a coupla times."

"Great."

Pumping iron together, Jilly Coombes said, "Maybe I could come over and spend a week with you. Sleep on the couch. Drink some beer."

Ben said, "Fine," but Jilly's parents said no. They suspected mischief.

Alfredo also had a knowing look on his moon face: Hokay, *señor*, big boss gone, we'll have some fun.

Ben often ate with the Garcias.

Graciela's pork tacos and veal and chicken sausages, with chiles and cilantro, were sensational.

When his parents had first announced the African trip, Ben *had* been truly glad. Breathing room, at last.

And Alfredo was there to handle any emergencies. He'd been in the United States for sixteen years, half his life. Born in Durango, Mexico, he'd first sneaked across the border east of Tecate; worked strawberries, then asparagus. Stoop-work. Finally, he drove plows and cultivators. But then the Jepsons had offered good housing plus steady pay. Alfredo had been at the preserve since it opened.

Housing, without living with another Latino family, was very important to Alfredo and Graciela. In Durango, they'd lived in dirt-floored huts with tin roofs. Now they lived in the middle of the compound, with two small children, in a nice mobile home.

Alfredo and Graciela were about to become citizens under the new amnesty act. They'd learned to speak softly accented English. There was strong mutual affection between Ben and the Garcias.

The last thing that Peter Jepson had said to Ben and Alfredo before entering the British Airways 747 for the flight to London and then on to Nairobi, Kenya, was a cheerful, confident, "You two keep it in the road," but his mother, kissing his cheek lightly, added her usual cautionary, not-so-confident declaration to Ben. "Yeah, pal, but if you go into a ditch, call us, will you?" Typical.

"Okay, Ben?" Her green eyes were pinning him.

"Okay," Ben said. Call them in Tanzania?

That was his mother, year in and year out; day in, day out, it seemed to him. A few choice words of advice, peck on the cheek, toothy smile, somehow growing more remote each year. Internationally known photographer, pretty

Dorothy Courtney-Jepson, in her Bill Blass sports jacket and Cacharel silk blouse, Fendi boots and Calvin Klein gabardine slacks, smelling of expensive perfume. Stunning mother, sharp-tongued mother.

Loving mother?

About the time the punk rocker climbed the perimeter fence, when Ben was twelve, he'd found and read an unfinished letter to his grandmother on her desk. Never had he done that before — read someone else's mail — but somehow he was drawn to those sheets of paper addressed to Grandmother Deedee Courtney.

On the second page was this paragraph:

"I'm discouraged about Ben. He seems so mediocre and has no drive except a physical one. He tries to play Pony League and isn't very good. Tries to surf and isn't very good at that, from what I hear. His grades are awful. Mediocre is all I can say. Such a disappointment. I think he could be one of these kids who just doesn't have it upstairs. Peter isn't nearly as concerned as I am. Yes, I'd like Ben to go to Stanford or Yale or Harvard. Peter's attitude is that everyone isn't college material and Ben will find himself. I hope so. I doubt it. Right now, he's a prime candidate for a ten-dollar-an-hour job as an animal trainer."

Feeling as though he was going to throw up, Ben ran out of the house and went to the compound where two-year-old Rocky lived. They went for a long walk along the Naranja, Ben telling the lion about the letter and a lot of other things that were on his mind like joining the Marines

in five years and never coming back to Los Coyotes except
to visit his dad.

"And you, Rocky!"

Ben didn't ask his mother about the damning letter or
tell his father. It was one of those things he lived with, a
stony ache inside him whenever he thought of it. Later,
he told Jilly Coombes about the letter; then Sandy. They'd
frowned and winced, not knowing quite what to say. Mediocre? Jilly had finally said, "Well, if you are, I am too."

And Sandy said, "Count me in."

Also on the wall in Ben's room were photos of Sandy,
in her bikini, down by the lake, and Jilly and Ben in their
Pony League football uniforms, signed Dorothy Courtney-
Jepson. None of Alfredo. What she didn't know was that
there were photos of Ben and Alfredo in Alfredo's mobile
home, taken by Graciela.

People often looked at Dorothy Courtney-Jepson in air-
ports, with all of her cameras she never checked through, or
when she was anyplace else, for that matter. Men one way;
women enviously. There was a "Who's she?" celebrity aura
about her.

Ever since establishing the preserve, one of Ben's parents had always stayed home when lengthy overseas trips
were involved. Since they worked as a team, father doing
research and writing, mother doing photography, it wasn't
a very good way to operate. After Peter Jepson came home,
Dorothy'd fly off to do the pictures, anywhere in the world.
They teamed on best-selling books and did the town hall
lecture circuits individually; often TV talk shows together,
smiling, laughing, always at ease. Ben had watched them,
shaking his head. They were so tuned to each other.

But now that he was almost fifteen, they finally felt they could go as a team.

Peter Jepson did look the part of an adventurer-scientist, with a short pepper-and-salt beard, perpetual tan, and deep-set blue eyes; he looked like a skier or mountain climber. In addition to being an internationally known zoologist, he was a fine writer. Ben figured he'd inherited his dad's eyes. That's all. Not his looks, not his size, not his brains, not his courage. Certainly not his courage. Who else could go in with Dmitri?

His mother, always wearing her hair cut short so wind wouldn't blow it across the camera lenses, looked a little like the actress Candice Bergen, except she was taller, six feet, almost as tall as Ben's father. Ben couldn't figure out what he'd inherited from her and worried that she'd always be taller than he was. She'd be looking down on him when he was twenty-one. He was destined to be a runt, he thought. He'd move to the East Coast.

Before they left on this trip, Ben's dad had drawn up a list of chores and things to do in an emergency. June was the beginning of the fire season in southern California. He wrote down names of cattle truckers to move the animals, just in case an evacuation was necessary.

Then he wrote down the regular contacts like Dr. Larry Templeton, their longtime vet, specialist in exotic animals; Al Levine, the meat supplier.

"*Rutina*," said Alfredo, shrugging. *Routine*. Ben echoed him, laughing and shrugging. Up, up and away.

Ben had seen some of his father's research for the trip: gangs of ex-Shiftas, old-time mercenaries, were hunting in parties from twenty to eighty people, all armed, some with machine guns, going after elephant tusks, leopard and chee-tah skins. There was heavy poaching in the Mugumu, Ikoma, and Mbalageti-Duma areas.

So there was much more danger over there, and as they started down the ramp to the 747, he'd yelled, "Be careful."

They'd smiled and waved, his mother blowing a kiss, like a movie scene.

He'd told them to stop off in London on the way back, see some plays. Don't worry about Los Coyotes.

And off they went to do their article for the *National Geographic.* His dad was on an angry crusade against the poaching, which had taken twenty thousand leopard skins out of Africa in the last five years. Big money involved. Park rangers had been shot at by the poachers, and even impoverished tribesmen had killed intruders, such as Dor-othy and Peter Jepson, with poisoned arrows.

Because they had to pick up an animal that day from Dr. Templeton on the way home, his dad had driven the cat wagon, an old, faded green delivery-type van, to Los An-geles International, Ben and Alfredo riding in the back, talking and laughing.

The van was used to haul the cats around, and there was a welded chain-link barrier behind the passenger and driver bucket seats, steel bars over the side windows. Grown lions and tigers, fearful of being removed from their homes, were never ideal cargoes. Not even cubs were al-lowed to sit with the driver. Only a dignified cheetah like Rachel was allowed front-seat privileges in the '71 Dodge with CAT WAGN on the license plate.

Alfredo was a Willie Nelson fan and had converted

Ben. They sang along with Willie all the way to the vet's: "Mammas Don't Let Your Babies Grow Up to Be Cowboys" and "Good Hearted Woman" and "Blue Eyes Crying in the Rain," and others on the cassette. Old wrinkled Willie *nose-singer* with his braids and red bandanna and overalls, without a shirt. What a time!

Cowboys ain't easy to love,
and they're harder to hold,
They'd rather give you a song
than diamonds or gold . . .

Lone Star belt buckles and old faded
Levi's and each night begins a new
day . . .

If you don't understand him, he don't
die young, he'll probably just ride
away . . .

Mammas don't let your babies grow up
to be cowboys . . .

Don't let 'em pick guitars and drive
an old bus; let 'em be doctors and
lawyers and such . . .

Mammas don't let your babies grow up
to be cowboys. They'll never stay
home and they're always alone,
even with someone they love . . .

Waylon Jennings and old Willie were singing that song as the CAT WAGN headed home, Ben deciding he was the cowboy.

Now Alfredo, who'd taught Ben to pick guitar, was in intensive care, fighting for his life, and The Sisters were dead.

Nothing at all routine this early June morning.

Ben's school friends couldn't get over where he lived, how he lived. Who else his age awakened to the bellowing of big cats? Heard them bumping against the bedroom wall at night? Could throw covers back and see a living, breathing Bengal tiger ten feet away? Walk across the Rio Naranja and be in an artificial savanna?

In their living room, in scrapbooks, were photos of a curly-headed boy sleeping contentedly alongside an equally contented half-grown lion. There were other photos of Ben with the big cats, taken at ages eight and older. Some of his earliest memories were of the beige-gold animals on the African plains; him sitting spellbound in a Land Rover while his dad drove slowly past lazy prides of them. He'd known cats a long time.

He'd been to the Serengeti twice; first as a two-year-old, then when he was six. They'd lived at Seronera, park headquarters, while his father observed and tagged lions, his mother photographing them, going out almost every dawn. They bumped around in the Land Rover and slept in tents.

Through binoculars: "Now, watch, Ben, that lion is grimacing at us. See, his mouth is open, his canines are bared, his upper lip pulled back. He looks ferocious, but he's only sniffing. He has two holes in the roof of his mouth to help him do that. His sense of smell is very poor."

Ben was forever hearing, "Remember that time in Gorongosa, that pride living in that old house . . ." or the story about the lioness jumping up on the roof in Wankie, staying there. Or the giraffe that raced the Rover in Ngorongoro.

But the African travel ended the year Ben met Reggie. A rich widow in Florida, a big cat lover, offered to permanently endow a place to study and breed the animals in captivity. So the Jepsons traveled all around the Southwest to locate land that would look and feel like parts of the Serengeti.

They found it below Los Angeles, in Orange County, a movie animal-trainer's ranch, the giant brown boulders looking a lot like the granite and gneiss *kopjes* of the African savanna.

With the endowment money, Ben's parents bought the hundred-ninety-five acres, canyon country pierced by the lazy little Rio Naranja, dotted with those huge boulders, the *kopjes*, big blue oaks and dozens of towering cottonwoods. Had the trees been thorny types or acacias, the acres would have resembled the African riverine woodlands almost exactly.

Rocky's Story

Thinking that Rocky could have been gunned down this morning just as easily as Helen and Daisy, Ben went over to Number Two compound to take a look at the road from there, believing that all the cats in the outer row might be in danger if the shooter came back. He was definitely not prepared to handle losing Rocky. He loved that cat like a brother, even though there were problems with him now.

Rocky saw him and rose up, coming to the fence to lick the back of his hand, Chico and Mikey staying down on all fours but looking intently his way.

Ben said, "I'm going to make sure no one shoots you, buddy."

Ben well remembered Rocky as a baby, well remembered what had happened five years ago: moody Roxanne abandoning her cub a few days after birth, leaping to the top of her den house, ignoring the cries of the infant they'd named Rocky.

Ben's dad said he thought Roxanne lacked milk, but no human could have touched her teats to prove it. She simply shut her ears to the high-pitched hunger screams. So they didn't argue with her; didn't tell her she was being a bad mother—a waste of words. Instead, his dad had said, "Cub's all yours, Ben. Good luck, boy. You'll certainly need it."

Neither Ben nor his dad could know that little Rocky was a time bomb.

So, ten-year-old Ben became the surrogate "mother," force-feeding the foot-long cub puppy formula through a tube every two hours around the clock.

"Don't let it go down his windpipe or he'll get pneumonia. He'll die in less than an hour," advised his dad.

Ben sweated every feeding.

"Maybe you should give up," said his mother.

"He *has* to live," said Ben. "He *must* live."

After two sleepless weeks, Ben's dad said, "Okay, let's try KMR," and the tiny, woolly, yellow-gold animal was finally persuaded to accept Kitty Milk Replacement, a zoo standby, through a preemie nipple.

But from his fifth night on earth, Rocky slept beside Ben's head, constantly seeking reassurance, making the lion cub's usual "Where are you?" sound. If Ben left the bed and didn't carry Rocky along, he'd soon hear an "aa-aow," the sound that would someday become a roar.

Ben's mother said, "You should have been a girl. I've never seen such a maternal instinct."

Ben didn't quite know how to take those words and laughed hollowly in return.

Bluish film coated Rocky's eyes at birth, but a week later the film vanished, and he could see though he couldn't focus. When focusing finally occurred, Ben was the first human imprinted on the cub. So far as Rocky was concerned, then and forever, Ben was his *father-mother* rolled into one.

Frowning a little, worrying about the future, Ben's dad had said, "You have a devoted son, for better or worse."

For weeks, Ben bottle-nursed Rocky, belly down on his lap, spotted, petal-eared head pointed toward his knees, right hand crooked to hold the bottle. He burped the tiny cub with a towel over his shoulder, human-style; held him as if he were a human baby; cooed to him.

So began the love affair between Benjamin Jepson and Rocky Lion.

Tongues of adult lions are like rasps, useful in cleaning meat off bones, useful in grooming each other, and Rocky's little tongue was already rough. Ben's thumb became tender as the cub sought it for a substitute mother's nipple. Rocky was at Ben's heels everywhere he went, sometimes nipping them, always wanting to play.

Young Ben took him to school, his own and then others, and became a sort of celebrity. He made appearances with Rocky in shopping malls and children's hospitals. The Los Angeles TV stations and newspapers loved the freckled blond boy with the cute lion cub.

The time bomb was ticking away.

A Neighbor?

Placing a call to Seronera, on the Mukoma Plain, fifty minutes by small aircraft from Nairobi, Ben knew it was likely his parents wouldn't be at park headquarters. But he thought there'd be radio contact with them out in the bush. They were operating from a Land Rover, camping out.

It was 6:40 A.M., California time, late afternoon East Africa time. He had rehearsed what he was going to say after asking how they were: "Alfredo was in an automobile accident and is in intensive care . . . we've got a poacher right here . . . Helen's dead . . . Daisy's dead . . . shot in the heart. . ."

Then he wanted to ask whether or not he should call Deputy Metcalf, Larry Templeton, the neighbors, Animal Control. Things were sticky with the latter two, with the exception of the Gilmores, and had been for some time. What should he do? He didn't want them to rush home, just give him some good guidance. Truthfully, he did want them to rush home. Right now. The idea of coping with someone who was letting cats out, shooting cats, and of running the preserve suddenly seemed a cliff too high to climb.

A female voice came up in Seronera saying that the director was in Rome but maybe the Chief Park Warden could help. She sounded British.

"Yes, please," Ben said.

In a moment, the warden came on, and Ben identified himself as the son of Dr. and Mrs. Jepson, who were working in the Serengeti, saying he needed to contact them—an emergency.

"Well, we haven't heard from them in four days. I don't think anything is wrong, however. They're somewhere past Kirawira, west of us, near the park boundary. Radio reception isn't very good this week due to sunspots, and I can't say our equipment is the best." He sounded a little like Hudson Odinga.

"I really need to talk to them," said Ben.

"All right, we'll try to rouse them at the dinner hour," the warden promised. "They're guarding our frequency, I think. I'll tell them to call you."

"Please," Ben said, desperation clearly in his voice.

Who opened the main gate, the compound gates, fired the shots? The neighbors?

George Trilby?

One of rich Mrs. Mesko's hired hands? Crusty Mrs. Mesko herself?

Old man Carpenter? Twist Carpenter?

Richie Lewis?

Ben immediately suspected George Trilby or Richie, but the others might have thought they had reasons, as well.

"How many animals are you going to have?" George Trilby had casually asked when his father introduced himself at Trilby's country store soon after they bought the property. Ben, aged nine, was along that spring day.

"Oh, ninety or a hundred lions, tigers, leopards, cougars, jaguars," his dad said, smiling widely, not thinking about the impact of such numbers. Zoologists tend to think in terms of entire species, hundreds of animals.

After Ben and his dad had driven away, they later learned, Trilby called the county animal regulation people, finding out that the required permit had been granted. Trilby then called neighbors—the Meskos, the Lewises, the Amos Carpenters, the Gilmores—Peter also learned, asking them to sign a petition.

"This lunatic is talking about a hundred lions and tigers. That's more than at the San Diego Zoo," the grocer supposedly told them. "We can't have those people here."

The only friendly neighbors, it seemed, were the Gilmores, whose small ranch was dwarfed by the Meskos' ten thousand acres. Though the Gilmores owned three horses, it wasn't a working ranch. Mr. Gilmore was an accountant, and Mrs. Gilmore sold real estate. They refused to sign Trilby's petition after discovering the Jepsons had a legitimate permit. They had a daughter, Sandra, and two sons.

His dad believed that Trilby, who was around forty, a gaunt, long-faced man, was concerned primarily about the strip of land he owned between the preserve and the Golden Years trailer park. Those acres butted on the Lewis property as well. Trilby hadn't been able to sell them while the movie trainer lived there in his trailer, ". . . those damn wolves of his howlin' every night."

Now he probably thought he'd never sell his land—all those lions roaring, leopards barking.

Trilby had a snippy daughter, Julie, and she came up to Ben the second or third day of school to say, "You're the new boy from that private zoo, aren't you?"

Ben protested, "It isn't a zoo. It's a place for research."

"Whatever it is," she said, "a lot of people don't want it here." Her father didn't, for certain. She never spoke to Ben again.

The *Orange County Register* didn't help with a story headlined: *Jet-Setting Zoology Couple to Host a Hundred Big Cats.* "The Peter Jepsons, called 'beautiful people' by *People* magazine, will have their own private zoo in Los Coyotes Canyon . . ."

At the time, a few months after purchase, with Ben's dad often manning the bulldozer and bossing the fencing crew, building the preserve, landscaping it, they had only a half-dozen cats, including Reggie, bought from the former owner of the land. His mother said, "Maybe we should try to find another place. Everyone here seems to be against us."

"Don't even think about it," his dad replied angrily. "We're legal! We're staying! That's that!"

They well knew how stubborn he could be at times.

Ben was glad his dad would fight back.

Then there was the messy survey problem. Before putting in the fourteen-foot-high steel-link, butting the Lewis property, his dad had all hundred-ninety-five acres surveyed. Transits revealed that the Lewis property had been incorrectly fenced. The Lewis line of posts and waist-high barbed wire, to keep their cattle in, encroached fifty-six feet into preserve property for almost a quarter of a mile. Informed by the surveyor, Ben's father was ready to let the Lewises keep the land for the sake of better relations.

The next morning they went over to inspect the new stakes, taking Jessica, a mild-mannered castoff from a circus, with them. The compounds still weren't completed, and the animals were still in small cages, so exercising was important. They went through a Lewis gate to get to the new markers and were inspecting them when Richie, Jack Lewis's only son, a big guy in his mid-twenties, drove up in a dusty Jeep, shouting, "You're trespassin', jackass. Git off our property an' take that wild animal with you. This is a cattle ranch, an' we don't want no lions on it."

His dad stared back at Richie, Ben remembered so very clearly, saying, "Mister, you've got a real bad mouth. You aware of that?" He'd stayed in pretty good shape since playing defensive end at the University of Virginia. Squash and a lot of tennis. At thirty-eight, he was still muscular.

"I'm aware you're on our land. Now git off!" Richie's ugly face belonged on Saturday night wrestling, Ben thought. He had a big, shaggy head.

His dad suddenly decided he'd stick to the newly surveyed stakes. "Your fence is fifty-six feet off. A new survey was completed yesterday. You're off fifty-six feet the whole distance."

"Survey's wrong, jackass. Now, take that lion an' march." Richie hadn't shaved in a good three days, Ben thought. He looked fearsome.

His dad was trying very hard to control his temper, Ben saw. "It seems to me we're on the inside of that stake down there and that one up there." He pointed both ways. "That's the line where our fence is going in, whether you like it or not."

"Bullllllll," said Richie, like one of his cattle baying.

"That stake's twenty feet on our side. Now git off our land, I'm sayin'."

Though he knew he might be making a mistake, he said later, Ben's dad didn't think it was time to run. Walking up to the Jeep, holding Jessica on the lead, he said, "We'd really like to be good neighbors but won't be pushed around, Mr. Lewis. This new survey is correct. Have your father call me for the surveyor's name and phone."

Richie laughed, shaking his head. "You jus' don't lissen, lion-tamer. We're gonna run you outta here."

Peter Jepson said, very quietly, "I'm giving you ten seconds to get that Jeep off our land. Just ten! I'll count in my head."

Richie's coarse, slack mouth dropped in astonishment, and his bloodshot eyes swelled. He reached down, turning off the ignition defiantly, throwing his long legs out simultaneously, saying, as his boots touched the ground, "Why, you orderin' me . . ."

Ben hadn't realized the size of Richie Lewis until he stood straight up. At least six-three, six-four. He'd weigh around two-forty, bigger than most NFL linebackers. His fists were already clenched.

Ben's heart drummed. He could barely breathe.

His dad said, steadily, "Five seconds, Mr. Lewis. I don't know what will happen when I turn this animal loose . . ."

He did know. Not one solitary thing. Nothing.

Jessica was looking out across the undulating fields of brown grass, paying no attention to human talk or tone of voice. If he'd let her off the lead, she'd probably flop down and begin grooming her paws. Jessica was a pussycat, though over three hundred pounds.

41

But Richie took a long look at the size of her and thought better about what he was doing. He turned and slid back into the Jeep, muttering, "We'll see 'bout this . . ."

The dusty Jeep spun around and bounced away, Ben's heart slamming.

The fourteen-foot-high perimeter fence went in exactly as staked, and the Lewises lost about four acres in total. They were enraged.

Not wanting to upset Dorothy, his dad didn't tell her about the encounter with Richie and swore Ben to secrecy too.

Work progressed rapidly.

The Los Coyotes property was shaped like a fat sweet potato, on a north-south line in the canyon, with the little river cutting through it. Only in California would the Naranja be called a river. In most places it was less than ten feet wide and only twelve or fifteen inches deep. But the mountain runoff was clear and clean, a place for the tigers to soak and sleep year-round, noses barely above water.

The fattest end of Los Coyotes was the northern extremity, and up there various support buildings were soon erected: a huge walk-in freezer for meat, mechanical shop, shed for the bulldozer and backhoe, a small animal hospital and a helicopter pad if visiting zoologists chose to fly in from Los Angeles International.

They had dammed the Naranja, and the resulting little lake was also on the north end, as were the handlers' quarters and three mobile homes for visiting scientists.

By year's end, they were settled into the old board-and-batten perched on the edge of the river. Condemned by the state for freeway clearance, Peter and Dorothy had bought it at auction. House movers had done the rest.

African big cat paintings by Kimathi and Indian tiger paintings by Prasdan covered the walls. Around the rooms were wooden carvings of animals by Mikandi and Lupali, Mogendi stone carvings from Kisii. It was a startling house. Even Sandy thought so.

The living room furniture—big wing-backed rattan chairs, a pair of huge sofas covered with soft woven throws from Mbala, and a large coffee table made of muswili wood—looked as if it might have come out of Aberdare's famed Treetops Hotel. Ben's parents had brought Seronera, Samburu, Marsabit, Tsavo, and Masai Amboseli, some of the many places where they'd worked, to the house by the Naranja.

They began to gather cats from everywhere, free of charge. Lions were always a surplus. Some were zoo over-flows. A lioness like Helen could produce a litter every three and a half months.

Soon, they were running an orphanage; then they bred the young strong cats, which resulted in cubs like Rocky.

At age nine, Ben wasn't too interested in Sandra Gilmore, though she was curious about the boy who lived with the lions. She was very pretty and the same age but, at nine, boys went around with boys, girls with girls.

He'd wave.

She'd wave back.

He saw her in school and she saw him, and they'd say "hi" to each other.

Neither one could guess that in five years the relationship would change; a wave and smile would become a kiss.

Meanwhile, Rocky grew rapidly, eighty pounds when he was six months old, and he still slept in Ben's room each night, sharing the bed. Ben's dad soon said it was past time that Rocky go out and stay with the other young cats, be a normal lion. Ben asked for a few months longer.

"Ben, what's happening isn't really very healthy. It's usually all right to have a one-man dog but not a one-man lion. There's potential danger if you're the only one who can handle Rocky. The rest of us could be threatened."

Ben said to himself, *That's nonsense. Rocky is different. He likes to romp and have fun. Never would he hurt anyone.*

His mother said, "That cat has to go. *It has to go.*"

At nine months, Rocky weighed one hundred and ten pounds and was four feet long, big as a Great Dane, and Ben's dad insisted that he go *now*.

"Right now!"

He was showing signs of sprouting a royal mane; tail tuft developing. Ben sadly took him out to Number Five to live with six other young lions. Rocky seemed to take it in stride.

Spending time each day with him, walking him along the Naranja, toward the Carpenters' Golden Years trailer park, telling the lion secrets of the day, the week, Ben talked to him earnestly as if he were human.

As they sat by the lake, bodies pressing against each other, young Rocky would take Ben's thumb into his mouth like in the old times when he was a cub. The tongue was no longer like sandpaper. It was a harsh rasp, but Ben willingly suffered the pain of their special relationship for a few minutes each occasion they took a walk. His thumb stayed raw.

Rocky was the brother Ben had never had, never would have.

Early one night, weeks after he'd read the letter to Grandmother Deedee Courtney, Ben had overheard a conversation between his parents. They were out on the porch having liqueurs and coffee. They obviously didn't know he was on the couch in the living room, reading. The window was open.

"Maybe we should send him to that school up in Santa Barbara? Cate, I think it's called."

"Why?" his father had asked.

"You see his grades today? They're on the table."

"I saw them."

"Two C's, the rest D's, and an F. He should be getting B's, at least. I can't believe *my* son is such a dumbo. He's either not studying, not concentrating, or he's not capable. I gave him a computer. Instead of learning how to operate it, he plunks country-western on that guitar. Plunks, not plays."

Silence from his mother. Probably taking a sip of Grand Marnier.

Silence from his dad. Probably taking a sip of Cherry Heering.

Then, "I fix him gourmet meals. He seems to prefer Graciela's enchiladas."

His dad laughed. "Aha, now we know. His taste buds are wrong."

"I'll give him an A for handling Rocky and doing manual chores around here."

"Dot, come on, he's very capable for his age. Give him a break. Does he have to be a high achiever at twelve?"

"He should be. That's what I want him to be, a high achiever. I was, you were. I had straight A's when I was his age."

"Congratulations. I didn't."

"You're defending him again, always defending."

"I love him."

"So do I," she said, "and that's exactly why I say we should send him to Santa Barbara so he can learn how to study, associate with boys with a higher IQ than Jilly Coombes; get him away from Alfredo's influence . . ."

"Well, I'm not sure that's how I want to show my love, sending him off. And I'd like to know what's wrong with Alfredo?"

"Number 1, he's a simple Mexican. Number 2, he's a hired hand. Number 3, he thinks like a hired hand. I want Ben to think like the boss man."

"Honest to God, Dot, you have such a superiority complex."

"And, my darling, I'm proud of it."

Ben wanted to jump out on the porch and yell at her, "Alfredo's a good man, a kind man; he teaches me, gives me bear hugs," but was afraid of the steel-rimmed words she'd say back. So he slid off the couch and went to his room, tossing himself on the bed, not turning on the light. He was awake when his mother opened the door to say good night but faked being asleep.

He never did go to Santa Barbara, thanks to his father. That year he turned twelve seemed ancient history now.

The birthday computer was still in his room up against the far wall, gathering dust. Three years of gathering dust. He hated it. The big glass eye seemed to stare at him every time he went in or out, making him feel guilty. He thought it stared at him when he slept. Sometimes he'd fire it up and tap out some four-letter words on the screen.

Well, just because everybody else was ga-ga over computers didn't mean he had to join them. He once sent a message to the Apple II instructing it to self-destruct.

He wasn't quite sure why he hated the Apple II so much. Maybe it was because of the message his mother was sending with it: BEN, GO TO YALE.

Once, he tapped out, MOTHER, GO TO HELL, and then repeated it two thousand times on a loop, grinning at the green screen. There, that served her right.

But over in the corner was the beat-up Palmer guitar that Alfredo had bought for twelve dollars at a swap meet for the same birthday. He'd taught Ben about notes and chords and skinny strings and fat strings; how to hold the guitar and strum the skinny strings. He'd taught him keys and two-chord tunes and three-chord tunes. He'd even taught Ben a few *corridos*, Mexican country-westerns.

They'd sat out at that telephone company spool table in Alfredo's front yard doing "Ida Red" and "Rye Whiskey," two-chorders; then three-chorders like "Devil in a Sleeping Bag" and "Mammas Don't Let Your Babies Grow Up to Be Cowboys," Alfredo doing Waylon's part and Ben doing Willie's.

It was a lot more fun for him to play the Palmer than it was to play the Apple. Why couldn't she realize that?

Why did she always make him feel that he was letting her down? What was her reason?

"Why?" Ben asked his dad one night when she was in New York shooting a fashion layout.

His father sighed. "That's just the way she is, and you'll have to live with it. She'll never change, Ben. Deedee said she hasn't changed much since she was a little girl, always wanting to be Numero Uno. Nothing much wrong with that. It's one of the reasons I married her."

"But why me? Why do I have to be Number One too?"

His father took his time in answering. "You're it. You're her shooting star. She couldn't have any more children after you. You know that."

"That's not my fault."

"Who said it was? Look, she loves you. She really does. She cares deeply about you. She just shows it in a different way."

"Which way?"

His father took another long time in answering. "Her concern about you as a whole person."

"Not just my grades?"

"Not just your grades."

Whole person?

Richie Lewis?

Although Ben saw him driving by now and then in his white pickup or saw him at work over on the Lewis ranch, the Jepsons didn't come face-to-face with Richie until ten months after the fence incident. That time it was on the dirt parking lot of The Q. T. Bar, better known as The Cootie Bar, on past the sheriff's substation. Richie was rolling out of The Cootie all beered up on a Saturday afternoon, and Ben's dad was going in to buy a couple of six-packs for the handlers.

Ben was there that day, sitting in the cat wagon.

Richie said something, turned and took a swing at Peter Jepson.

It missed.

Ben's dad then hit their neighbor in the gut harder than he'd ever hit a big cat or a human, the latter not since his football days, the former not since a jaguar jumped him. It was a vicious punch, and Richie collapsed on all fours.

Peter stood over him, asking, "You want more?"

Richie didn't answer as Ben's dad went on into The Cootie.

Ben saw that Richie was puking. He'd carried that picture in his head to this day, the big body on all fours.

Then Ben remembered Alfredo's first encounter with Richie not long after he'd come to work at the preserve. They'd gassed up the cat wagon at the Arco station, and Alfredo was checking the tires when Richie came along in his pickup.

Recognizing the vehicle, he'd started honking, leaning his head out the window to shout, "Hey, Messican, git that van outta the way."

Alfredo had replied, "*Momento*, mister," taking his time in checking the last tire.

Richie unraveled from the pickup and came to stand over Alfredo's squatting form. "Want me to move it for you?" he asked threateningly.

Alfredo rose up. Though he was half a head shorter than Richie, the bigger man couldn't help but notice the heavy shoulders, thick neck, and bulging arms of the Mexican.

Richie mumbled something and got back into his truck.

He was a *valentón*, a *bully*, Alfredo said to Ben, and someday . . .

Ben also remembered the evening when Graciela had called from that same Arco station saying she'd been forced off the road. She wanted to know if it was okay to hire the Arco rig to tow her out of the ditch. The kids were with her.

"You all right? Children okay?" Alfredo had asked.

She said no one was hurt.

"How did it happen?"

"Some drunk went over the line, almost hit me head-on."

"Where is the car?"

"About two miles east of the station."

"Let Max tow you out. I'll be up," said Alfredo.

Later, Graciela told him that the drunk was driving a white pickup.

"Richie Lewis?"

She nodded.

Alfredo had sworn to Ben that at the right time and proper place Richie would pay. But Alfredo wouldn't be out of the hospital for days or weeks.

Had Richie fired the shots?

Shifting Cats

Ben called Sandy. "Someone let the cats out early this morning. They killed Helen and Daisy."

"What?" Ben could see her sunny face, brows furrowed, disbelief in the wide frown, the open mouth.

He repeated what he'd said.

"Why would anyone do that?" He knew she was shaking her head, appalled.

"I don't know, Sandy. I've been thinking about it for the last three hours. Someone who knows us, I guess. Someone who hates the cats." Richie Lewis?

"Have you called the sheriff?"

"Not yet. I'm going to in a few minutes."

He could hear her telling her parents. They were probably having breakfast. Then he heard Mr. Gilmore talking in the background.

"Is there anything my father can do?" Sandy asked.

"I don't think so. I'll talk to you later."

"Call me at the pool if you find out anything."

He said he would.

Sandy was Ben's first and, to this point, only steady girlfriend. Swimmer and horse lover, she often visited the preserve, riding her mare up, parking it at the front gate, then walking down into the canyon. Horses and big cats didn't mix. Sometimes she rode her ten-speed the three miles from her house to the preserve. She knew the cats, knew Helen and Daisy.

She was a sunshine girl, blonde with a trim tanned body but brown eyes instead of blue. She described her nose as "re-troo-say," a French word, she said. Partial pug, Ben decided.

This summer she was working six days a week as a lifeguard at the Coto de Caza Country Club kiddie pool.

Next Ben phoned Jilly Coombes, but Jilly had already gone off to work at McDonald's on Bridger Road in El Toro.

Finally, he put a call in for Harry Metcalf at the Santiago Canyon Substation, Orange County Sheriff's Department. Friendly, low-key, he was investigative deputy for the area in which the preserve was located. He'd been summoned in the past when the crazies visited. Ben liked him. Stubby and crew cut, an ex-Marine, he wore string ties and off-the-rack summer-weight sports jackets year round. But underneath the loud cotton jackets was a Smith & Wesson .38 in a shoulder holster. Deputy Metcalf wasn't at the station, but the operator said she'd have him call.

By 9:00 A.M. the phone still hadn't rung from Seronera, and the dinner hour over there had now passed. Ben had to believe it was just bad communications that prevented his parents from calling. Perhaps they'd call during the night, West Coast time. He hoped so.

Almost panicky, fearing another shooting, he told Luis

and Rafael that they'd have to shift some of the cats that lived in the outer compounds to safer quarters in the row to the east. Most of the outer compounds could easily be targeted from the road. Those cats, except Dmitri, were exposed. Dmitri's compound was behind a low hill.

He thought that's what his dad would do; what Alfredo would do. Shift the cats.

Ben explained to Luis, "We have to be careful which cats go into what compounds. You can't mix Bruno with Sammy, put Raymond in with Bobby. They'll fight."

Luis translated to Rafael.

There were other bad mixes to be considered in this emergency switch. They'd also have to shift some of the lionesses, including those females on birth-control pills. The breeding program had stopped after Rocky was born because of overcrowding. The lionesses would go in with the tigers, except Dimmy, making room for lions. There were problems in doubling up the females. Several were not at all sisterly. Chelsea was a she-devil. Some of them could be walked peacefully on leads while others had to be channeled through chutes or portable fencing.

Luis and Ben worked with long hog-handler canes to guide the cats around. Roaring, Judy charged Ben in a cloud of dust when he prodded her in the ribs. "Yah," he shouted, and she loped into the chute like a yearling.

Sasha tiger raised a paw at Rafael, causing him to shout, "¡Qué ruso tan engañoso!" *You phony Russian!* Sasha skedaddled on through the chute.

Herbie sat down in the chute to scratch at his head with a hind paw, like a dog. "Do that on your own time," Ben yelled, using his cane to send the lion on his way.

Telling Rafael and Luis to take a break, Ben personally moved Rocky to his new quarters.

Rafael was from Chihuahua, Luis from Albuquerque. Both single, they shared the small Airstream trailer. Both in their mid-twenties, Rafael didn't have a work permit, nor did he qualify for amnesty, and was as illegal as a cherry bomb from Tijuana. Ben's dad had taught Alfredo, who was afraid of big cats at first, and then Alfredo taught a succession of Latinos, some of whom quit the first, second, or third days. Rafael and Luis had been at the preserve for less than a year. They were Alfredo's students.

Routing the animals to safer quarters took Ben's mind off Helen and Daisy for a while. There was the usual amount of snarling and snapping as on any moving day, reminiscent of circus cats going into the ring, playing their usual game with the whip-popping "tamer." The animals were never certain where they were being sent and therefore jittery. They were controlled by shouting and arm-waving; by the hog canes or, finally, by Hot-Shots, electric cattle prods. When real trouble developed, the fire extinguishers were used.

Within seconds of being herded into the chute, Bruno and Jo-Jo locked together, pyramiding, rising face-to-face on hind legs, a thousand pounds in motion, thrashing against a side, collapsing it, rolling away, coming loose to stand up and ready for another pyramid.

Their guttural roars echoed through the preserve while Ben shouted to Luis to get the cattle prods.

He broke his cane over Bruno's head, which was cocked to one side, exposing white canines that looked like crocodile fangs. Their wiry manes were standing on end.

Fights between two fully grown big cats were horrendous, even to experienced handlers, and comparative newcomers such as Rafael and Luis often quit when they broke out. But Luis came running back with two Hot-Shots, tossing one to Ben. They goosed the cats and quickly got leads around them, moving Bruno well away from Jo-Jo.

Ben went back to the house to check the answering machine while the handlers repaired the chute.

Waiting near the redwood porch with his wheelbarrow, rake, and shovel was a sad-faced Enrique Castillo, the maintenance man. Part Indian, his skin was the color of rich clay. When he smiled, which was often, his face was radiant. Anybody could just say "Ricky," and there was the wide smile, shining teeth. This morning, though, he was near tears over The Sisters.

Ricky was crippled from a bone set improperly when he was a child, but to the cats he was just a different type of wounded gazelle or impala or wildebeest. He was always talking to the big cats, grinning at them, thinking they loved him because they tracked along the fences when he limped by. What was in their eyes was not love. To them, Ricky was just a potential meal. No more.

Ben's dad had said to Ricky, "Never go into a compound when an animal is in there. Never."

On the compound fences were little wooden plaques showing a hand with a finger missing, reminders never to stick a finger in to be licked. Fingers were sometimes considered dessert. Ricky always put the back of his hand up to be tongued while he talked to the cats. Then he'd hobble on, watched with every crooked step.

Ricky kept saying to Ben, "*Apenado, apenado*, Benhamin." *Sorry, sorry.*

No calls from Seronera on the machine as yet, and Ben phoned Dr. Templeton. He was with a patient. That could be anything from a monkey to an elephant. His reception girl said she thought the doctor would be able to return the call within half an hour.

Besides being the cats' doctor, Larry Templeton was a good friend of the family. He and his wife came over often to have dinner, play bridge. But by the time Larry called, Ben had already made up his mind to go to the sheriff's department, not wait for Metcalf to return his call.

"Helen and Daisy shot? I can't believe it," said Larry.

Ben said, "It happened . . ."

"In the darkness?"

"Pitch black."

"Any idea who did it?"

"One of the neighbors, maybe. I'm going to the sheriff's." He said he thought that's what his dad might do, what Alfredo might do.

"Absolutely," Larry agreed. "Have you tried to get your folks?"

"I have a call in to them."

"Do you want me to come over and stay with you tonight?"

"I'll be fine." Sad but fine. Brave it out in the darkness.

"Call me if you need me."

Ben said he would. But Larry was a busy man. Ben hated to bother him.

If either of The Sisters had clawed someone, bitten someone, then there might have been the reason of revenge. But they were innocent, Ben knew. Whoever had killed them had done it for another reason. What was it?

Deputy Metcalf

Luis said, "You think Richie Lewis did it?" Luis was driving the CAT WAGN.

Ben said, "Maybe. But I don't know how he found out that my parents were gone and that Alfredo was in the hospital."

Luis snorted and shook his head.

Ben said, "He's had it in for us for a long time," and told Luis what happened when they surveyed the property, the fight in The Cootie Bar parking lot, and trouble twice with Alfredo.

Rachel was with them, sitting between the bucket seats, looking out.

The Jepsons had acquired her from a stockbroker in Tucson, a woman who kept her on a backyard chain. Most uncatlike of all cats, a captive black-spotted cheetah usually preferred human companionship to that of other felines. Rachel was that way, sometimes purring so loud in Ben's room at night that she awakened him. Her unhappy sound, seldom heard, was a high-pitched two-tone hum. At times, he felt Rachel was almost human, just like he felt Rocky was almost human.

The low hills on either side of the road were yellow, winter grass dry but still nutritious for the cattle. On either side of this section were tall, skinny eucalyptus. Usually Ben liked this desolate road in the eastern section of the county, out past Trabuco village. It was said that the 1800s bandit, Joaquin Murrieta, had galloped along here. There were sand and gravel pits, a long-abandoned gold mine, and the ruins of an ancient adobe that had once been a stagecoach stop. But Ben didn't take any pleasure from the drive this morning.

About eight miles up, they turned off at the Santiago Canyon Substation. The building was low, gray-shingled. Black and white patrol cars were parked around.

Deputy Metcalf had a cubbyhole office, and Ben walked in holding the bloody bullets, introducing Luis. Metcalf looked up, surprised, nodding to Luis, saying, "Ben, what . . .?"

Ben put the bullets down on Metcalf's desk.

Hudson Odinga had dug them out just before they rolled Helen and Daisy into the tarps.

"What're those for?" Deputy Metcalf asked, frowning down at them.

"The bullets that killed two of our lionesses early this morning."

"Someone shot them? Inside the fence?"

Ben nodded. "I think some guy stood up on the road and shot Helen and Daisy."

The deputy didn't know which animals they were. It made no difference.

"Early morning? Daybreak?"

"No, in the dark. About a quarter to five."

"Where are your mom and pop?"

"On a trip to Africa."

"Africa?" Metcalf said, frowning wider. "And you're out there alone? You're kidding."

"Alfredo is in Saddleback Hospital but Luis and another handler are with me. We've also got a man who's studying for his vet's license, Dr. Odinga. I'm okay."

"What are your folks doing so far away?" The deputy didn't approve.

"A story on poaching."

"Poaching? They do get around." He shook his head and then took a bullet between his fingers, murmuring, "Rifle, I think. I'll send them over to the lab in a few minutes." Then he looked up at Ben. "You see anyone with a gun?"

"It was pitch black, Mr. Metcalf. We didn't even know they were dead until we saw them in the grass. We didn't hear the shots."

Metcalf kept on looking at the slugs.

"They were good cats, Mr. Metcalf. Never harmed a soul."

"Any idea who might have done it?"

"Neighbors, maybe?"

"Neighbors? Come on!"

"A lot of people want us out of there, always have. Mrs. Mesko, Amos and Twist Carpenter. The Lewises. George Trilby. The Animal Control people."

"Animal Control doesn't go around shooting fenced lions."

"No one has ever really had cause to worry about our cats."

"They *have* gotten out," Metcalf reminded him.

"You can count the times on one hand."

"For some people that's enough," the deputy said, pulling a yellow tablet close to the desk edge, picking up a ballpoint. "Okay," he said.

Ben told him about the peacocks, finding two compounds open; waking up the handlers and Hudson Odinga; told him about getting all the cats back to their compounds except Helen and Daisy; then finding them.

"Why were they let out?"

"I don't know. Whoever did it knew enough to cut the wire to the alarm system on the front gate. The wire on top the perimeter fence, the one we had put in after that pink-haired girl climbed over, wasn't touched. So he came right through the main gate and walked down the road past Dmitri. He was smart enough to stay away from Dmitri. That Siberian would have had him for breakfast."

"Shame he didn't," said Metcalf, with a low half laugh.

Ben went on. "We didn't know the main gate was standing wide open until daylight. Whoever did it maybe thought the cats would come up that way, get up on the road. He'd shoot them up there."

"Were they in the clear?" Metcalf asked.

"In the clear?"

"Away from brush, trees, boulders?"

"They were in that high grass over from the lake, about two hundred feet down from the road," Ben said.

"Can you see the road from there, unobstructed?"

"Whoever shot them had a clear view of them. But how did he do it? It was so black out there that we couldn't even see each other."

"Passive night viewing device, I'd guess. They were

developed during Vietnam for special forces. I've heard the military has scopes that can boost light thirty-five-thousand to eighty-thousand times. Starlight scopes. Scopes that can be used to see with only stars for illumination. I've heard they've got night-vision binoculars that can spot a man in starlight at forty-five-hundred feet. High-tech stuff made right in this county."

"But he shot them in the heart. It was a bull's-eye, Hudson said. How could he be so accurate?"

"Expert marksman. If he had a good nightscope, two hundred feet . . . easy . . ." Metcalf's voice trailed off.

Ben shook his head. "I just can't imagine anyone wanting to kill our animals."

"Hunters do it all the time, Ben. They think nothing of it and get a thrill when they hit. In fact, there are hunters in this county who'd pay you people a lot of money just to get some shots at your cats. A lot."

"You think it's a hunter?"

Deputy Metcalf sighed. "Could be. Could be just some kook, some snuff-dippin' redneck wanting to practice with his new nightscope."

Ben blew out a breath. "That's scary."

Metcalf said, "All those guys are scary to me." He looked down at his tablet a moment, then raised his head again, eyes questioning. "Who knows your folks are gone?"

Ben was startled. "Not many people. Some close friends. Our vet, Dr. Templeton. The meat suppliers." He didn't know who they'd told.

"How about your friends?"

"Mine?" Ben was dumbfounded.

Metcalf nodded.

"A few know about it."

"That's all it takes, Ben. Just a few. They tell their parents, other friends. Pretty soon a lot of people know your folks are across the world."

That really hadn't occurred to Ben. Hadn't occurred to his parents, either, he was certain. They had no reason to think there'd be trouble. Otherwise, neither one would have left. *His friends?* Opening compounds, shooting cats? Sandy? Jilly? No way.

"Think about it," the deputy said. "Meanwhile, I'll ask some questions around about starscope owners, but if I were you, I'd shift any animals that can be seen from the road. For the time being. And I'd run some cheap bamboo fencing along those front compounds to hide the other cats."

"We shifted those in the exposed compounds about an hour ago." He hadn't thought about bamboo fencing.

"Good."

Going back to the preserve, Ben wondered again about who might have done it? Okay, Twist Carpenter and Ruth Mesko could be mean, vindictive women, but he couldn't believe they'd be prowling around in the dark, firing a starscope rifle. Old Amos Carpenter was in the same category. So he discounted all three.

Ancient, arthritic Jack Lewis wasn't likely to be out at 4:00 A.M., opening compound gates. They'd heard he was even having trouble driving. That left Richie Lewis and George Trilby. Trilby had his reason—that land he said he couldn't sell because of the cats. During those last few days of school, had Julie Trilby heard his folks were going away? Had she told her father?

Or was it Richie?

Even before his father's problems with Richie Lewis, there'd been trouble with him in the canyon country, dating back to Trabuco High days, and Papa Jack Lewis had always stood up for him, they'd heard.

Alfredo had warned Luis and Rafael to stay away from him.

Now that Ben thought about it, he realized that he'd heard Richie could fix deep-well pumps. So that meant he knew something about electricity, maybe enough to cut the exact wire on the main gate alarm system that would shut the whole thing off.

Yet he didn't want Richie to be the one.

The Carpenters

Luis stopped at the main gate so Ben could empty the rural mailbox. As usual, it was full. Letter from his mother's photo agent in New York; another from the paperback publisher back there; one from PBS in California; letter from the lecture bureau in Philadelphia for his dad. Bills, bills, bills. A huge stack of mail was rising in the office. He had instructions to send the bills to their accountant.

Soon as he entered the house, he again checked the answering machine.

Call for his dad from a Dr. Dimally at the University of Wisconsin; call from a Sacramento lawyer asking if he'd be an expert witness at an upcoming trial; another for him from the Elsa Foundation; one for his mother from an ad agency in New York. She also shot photos of animals for magazine ads. Fashions and cars. That famous one in all the slick magazines of a tiger leaping across an auto hood was hers. She'd used Sasha. A call from Merrill Lynch. Call from the insurance man.

Nothing on the black box from Seronera.

He dialed McDonald's on Bridger Road and asked for Jilly. It was noon, the busy time, but he still wanted to talk to Jilly.

Jilly had gotten his nickname when they were both about eight. At the time, Ben's friend never said anything in the millions. He went a step beyond. "There were jillions of bats in that cave," he'd say.

"Yeah," Jilly answered, when he got on the phone.

"You tell anyone my folks were going away?" Ben asked.

"Yeah," Jilly said.

"Who?"

"What's this all about?" Jilly asked, sounding annoyed.

"Who did you tell?"

"I can't remember who I told. What difference does it make?"

"Someone killed Helen and Daisy last night."

There was silence for a moment. Then Jilly said, also disbelieving, "What did you say?"

"You heard me."

There was a shouted, "Jilly, get off the phone," and he said, "I'll come over tonight."

Jilly also knew Helen and Daisy. Ben had taken him into the cat compounds plenty of times in the last six years. He'd spent the night now and then. Ben's parents liked him.

A year older than Ben, he was a red-haired guy with tremendous leg strength. Horsing around with a football, he'd often hit Ben so hard he thought his teeth had come loose. Jilly could be wild at times. They jogged and lifted weights together. Maybe that helped make them mediocre?

There were two or three other calls he could make, but this was a sunny late morning in June, and most people weren't home. So he decided to let them go until evening. Besides, despite what Deputy Metcalf had said, he just didn't think that any of his friends had other friends who'd shoot up animals.

He fixed ham and cheese on a kaiser bun for lunch, then ordered some bamboo fencing for pickup at four.

Metcalf arrived about one o'clock, saying, "Show me where you found them."

Ben walked him up there and pointed.

Blood was evident on the grass blades, and the imprint of Helen's body was still there. There'd been dew at 4:00 A.M., and the sun had dried the grass, making her imprint look like a mold.

The deputy scanned upward to the road. "Easy shot. He couldn't miss with a good scope."

Ben said, "I should have gone up there to look around."

"Maybe it was a good thing you didn't," said Metcalf. "Keep standing where you are. I want to take a look from up there."

He walked back to where he'd parked his gray unmarked sedan, near the cottage, and then drove it up on the road to a point opposite where Ben was standing inside the preserve.

Getting out of the car, Metcalf edged about eight feet down the embankment, going to within a few feet of the perimeter fence. He yelled, "I can see his buttocks' marks in the weeds here. Big guy." Richie Lewis? Ben asked himself.

Then Metcalf squatted down by the impression and

sighted an imaginary rifle at Ben, placing the barrel in one of the links at shoulder height from a sitting position. "He did it from here, all right."

The deputy stood up, looking around for empty shell casings or cigarette butts or any other evidence.

Finally, he shouted, "I'll call if I find out anything," then climbed into the gray car and drove off.

After Metcalf left, Ben worked up courage to go over and see the Carpenters. Alert them to the shooter. They weren't exactly friendly with the Jepsons but were still on speaking terms.

The Golden Years trailer park, where the average guest age was said to be sixty-eight, was connected to the Los Coyotes Preserve by the Naranja. The river flowed through both places, and the Carpenters, downstream, complained bitterly about lion pee in the water. But the county tested it and got a zero reading, as was expected. They still complained.

They were standing outside the trailer park office. Twist Carpenter, who had hair the color of deep red geraniums, white roots at the scalp, said, "Whoever did it, I'm glad they did." Though it was early afternoon, she was still wearing an orange housecoat and fluffy blue bedroom slippers. Ben had been told she spent all morning and early afternoon watching soaps.

Ben looked over at her. "They weren't hurting anyone, Mrs. Carpenter." *Be cool*, he told himself.

"Noise is bad enough, but the idea they're so close is worse," Amos said. He was a gnarled, bronzed little man with silken white hair. Lots of it. He was about half the size of Twist.

The well-kept park had ninety spaces, with complete hookups, a swimming pool fed by the Naranja, and a giant community TV dish. The spaces held everything from Open Road Minis to forty-thousand-dollar Komforts. Some renters were year-rounders, ignoring the summer heat. Others departed in late May for the mountains or Canada, returning in October.

"You haven't had any trouble in a long time, Mr. Carpenter," Ben said, realizing immediately it had been a mistake to come over and talk with them.

"Young man, that once was enough," said Amos. "Lookin' right out that window seein' a thousand-pound lion walkin' right through the park in broad daylight."

"The lions don't get that big, Mr. Carpenter, ever," Ben said. Dumb, dumb, dumb to come up and even try to talk.

"The hell they don't," said Amos. "I'da shot that one if I'da been able to get home an' get my gun." The Carpenters lived in a mobile home about sixty feet from their office.

Four years ago, a mellow old lion, Moses, had gotten loose and walked up along the riverbank. Ben had been in school when it happened. His dad went up and brought Moses home in the cat wagon. No one was hurt.

Ben said, "If you see anyone shooting or carrying a rifle with a scope on it, I'd appreciate you calling Deputy Metcalf at the sheriff's department."

Twist said, "If someone is shootin' lions, the sheriffs'll get no calls from us."

Ben saw Amos wink but didn't know what the wink meant.

He said good-bye as nicely as he could and drove back home. He'd been driving the CAT WAGN since he was twelve but only on the back roads. He was eligible for a learner's permit in July.

A message from Larry Templeton was on the machine: "Just checking to see how are you. Give me a ring, huh?"

Ben dialed right away.

"How's it going?" the vet asked.

"Things are confused."

"They will be for a few days."

"I can't get over what happened, seeing them down in the grass . . . dead."

"I know, Ben. I get a lot of sick animals in here, and some never leave on four feet."

"But these were shot to death."

"I've had some that were shot, too, so I know what it's like to deal with that kind of senseless act."

"I'm trying," said Ben.

"When you lose a close friend, you mourn them in a special way; then the thing to do is go out and find replacement friends. You've got plenty to choose from."

That was true. Some were quite like The Sisters.

"Let me know if you need me," said Larry.

Ben said he would. What he really needed was a call from the Serengeti; what he needed was Alfredo on his feet.

An Isolater High

It was true, he'd learned, running and lifting weights let you deal with problems without distractions. There was a separation of mind and body after you came up to speed. He could think better, clearer, while his legs were moving, pores pumping out sweat, hearing the pound of his feet at first, then losing that sound, reaching the usual runner's high after two or three miles. He'd started running with Jilly about the same time he'd started weights last year. But he wasn't in the mood to run this early afternoon. Maybe tonight?

Instead, he went to the weight shed, a windowless hut about fifteen by fifteen, once used as a storage place when the preserve was being landscaped. Fertilizer smells still clung to the plywood walls. The weight shed was his retreat, with a Schisler heavy-duty Olympic bench and a three-way power sled "Isolater" by the same company, isolating muscles to aid in running speed, jumping ability, and explosive starts. He'd need all three to play football. He bench-pressed Mondays and Thursdays, one day heavy, the other light, and used the power sled four times a week.

His father applauded when he bought the equipment with Jilly. Even his mother approved but said, "Hope you're not trying to be an Arnold Schwarzen . . . whatever his name is. That big idiot hunk in the movies."

Ben said it was for muscles and stamina. "Everyone is doing weights. Girls. Everyone."

Everyone was learning about deltoids and triceps and gastrocnemius and trapezius. Ben was trying to reach one-forty on the scales by August, start of football practice. He was hoping to make second-string this sophomore year at Trabuco High. He needed to be one-forty, at least, to compete. He was one-twenty-eight now.

"I'm doing it for my legs and to build weight," he'd said.

Nodding, she walked on to her darkroom that first day of the weights. She spent hours in there.

Well, he had no idea of becoming a Schwarzenegger or Mr. Universe. Those guys, posing with bunched muscles and veins like rubber tubing, were ridiculous, Ben thought. He didn't want to look like them. Why did she even bring that up?

Often the last three or four years he felt that there was a thick, soundproof glass wall between them. She could see him talking but couldn't hear the words. Didn't, wouldn't, couldn't.

Suddenly angry again at both of them for being away, not only his mother, he got on the Isolater to do some power squats, tandem weights behind his shoulders. Sucking in air, he started, feet firmly planted on the platform mat. The air hissed out, and the mind music began:

Cowboys like smoky old pool rooms
and clear mountain mornings; little
warm puppies and children and girls
of the night . . .

Them that don't know him
won't like him and them that do
sometimes won't know how to take
him . . .

He ain't wrong, he's just different
but his pride won't let him do things
to make you think he's right . . .

Mammas don't let your babies
grow up to be cowboys . . .

In many ways, his parents were so different from others that he just couldn't make any comparisons. Sometimes—no, often—he wished they weren't that different. Why couldn't they be more like the Coombeses or the Gilmores?

"You're overwhelmed by them, aren't you?" Sandy had said.

That was the right word. Overwhelmed.

He knew bits and pieces about them. They'd gotten together to do a book on the Serengeti lions, supported by a foundation grant, while his dad was a Smithsonian fellow. They'd fallen in love but didn't get married until Ben was two.

He remembered that when he was about seven, his mother said, smiling widely, "You know what? You're a love child, Ben, conceived on a cot under a bright moon at the Barafu Kopjes, in Kenya, a king of beasts roaring in the distance. *N'chi, ya nani? Yangu! Yangu! YANGU!"*

How could he forget that big YANGU?

What did all that mean, he'd asked.

"Whose land is this? Mine! Mine! MINE! That's the way you have to feel about life, Ben. Conquer it!"

Oh?

After she explained what conceived meant, he liked that story for a while, the part about the bright moon and the lion roaring in the distance at Barafu. Later, he had mixed feelings about it. But it was a secret shared by the three of them, he thought. Little bastard child.

And somehow the good genes had gotten lost. He often thought that the boy they conceived on that cot at the Barafu *Kopjes* could have been, perhaps should have been, the son of ten thousand other people, not Peter and Dorothy Courtney-Jepson.

They were alike in so many ways and so different in so many others that it was a wonder they ever agreed on anything. He'd said that to Grandmother Deedee Courtney, and she'd laughed. "Opposites attract, you know. Wouldn't it be dull if they were exactly alike?"

Dull? Exactly alike? Well, there was never a worry about that down in Los Coyotes Canyon.

What he wanted to say to Grandmother Deedee Courtney was, Why couldn't she be more like my dad? But he couldn't say that to Grandmother Deedee about her own daughter, either.

Did it take something out of her to be understanding? To see him as he was? Even mediocre. Was she afraid she'd have a meltdown if she put her arms around him now? He remembered her hugging him as a small child.

What was the ever-widening gulf between them?

It's ME—Ben Jepson—he'd finally decided a long time after that letter to Grandmother Deedee. Clearly, he hadn't lived up to her expectations as the letter had said. As if it had been engraved in stone, the letter wouldn't go away. Neither would her expectations.

Though he'd come out of her championship body, he didn't have the promise of a shooting star; he wasn't the thoroughbred who was going to win the Kentucky Derby for her; not a Rhodes scholar or an Olympic gold medalist. He was just a lonesome cowboy.

Cry an ocean.

Sweat was pouring down his face, puddling in the hollow of his neck; thigh muscles pulling and giving. He was getting into an isolater high.

His thoughts finally slid from his parents to George Trilby. He truly hoped George was the one. Above all, he didn't want Richie Lewis to be the shooter for the simple reason that he was still afraid of Richie after all these years. Raw fear in his head and in his gut. He still couldn't shake that morning when he was nine and his dad argued with Richie over the property lines; the scene in The Cootie parking lot, Richie down on his hands and knees. He'd avoided him, whenever possible, over the last six years. Maybe it was time to confront him. David and Goliath.

Mrs. Mesko

After the half-hour workout and a shower, Ben decided to go next door, warn Mrs. Mesko as well, ask for her help, though the two families hadn't spoken for most of the six years the Jepsons had lived there.

Not long after the preserve was being laid out, Ben's mother had stopped alongside the road when she saw Mrs. Mesko out on her horse. "Hi, I'm Dorothy Jepson, your new neighbor. Hope you'll come over and have a drink with us, see what we're doing."

"We know what you're doing and don't thank you for it," the ranch lady had tartly replied. She was a tall, angular woman with milk-white hair, clad in an expensive riding outfit, massive diamond ring on her left hand. She was a recent widow.

"We're as concerned about safety as you are," said Ben's mother. "Please come have a drink and we'll talk about it."

Reining around, Mrs. Mesko had practically shouted, "No, thank you."

Two years later Teddy lion had gotten loose during a shifting of the cats and had killed one of the Mesko champion Appaloosas. Ben's father had paid Mrs. Mesko eight thousand for the loss. The incident hadn't helped the relationship.

As Ben drove the CAT WAGN over the long tree-lined road up to the rambling one-story house, thin arms of water shooting from huge sprinklers out to the alfalfa fields on either side, he tried to rehearse what he planned to say to the old woman—if he could say anything. She might refuse to see him, he knew. But since he'd told the Carpenters, he thought he should also tell Mrs. Mesko.

Ben had seen the gray shingled house from the road many times and always wondered why it was so large for two people. Alfredo, who was friendly with Mrs. Mesko's foreman, said they'd built it for grandchildren to visit.

He rang the bell, and in a moment a Mexican girl answered the door. The maid, or housekeeper, Ben guessed. Old Mrs. Mesko had a lot of money. Cattle and crop money.

Ben said who he was and that he wanted to talk to Mrs. Mesko.

"*Momento*," said the girl, closing the door again.

In a moment she was back again, saying, "Come."

Ben followed her padding sandaled feet through a living room with huge white cowhide couches and a massive fireplace; through a dining room with a brown-stained wooden chandelier that had to be ten feet across; then out to the patio. Mrs. Mesko was seated out there at a glass-topped table.

Looking up, dark eyes rock-hard, she said, "What do you want?" Not hello—what do you want?

Ben said, "Two of our cats were shot last night."

Without changing expression, she asked, "What does that have to do with me?" Her nose was a beak.

"Whoever shot our cats could shoot your horses," Ben replied, fighting off intimidation.

The eyes wavered and narrowed. "Satan people? Those devil worshipers?"

"I don't know," said Ben. He hadn't thought about Satan people. They were animal mutilators, he'd heard.

"Did they come on the property?"

Ben nodded. "But they shot them from the road."

"Where are your parents?"

"Away for a few days," Ben said. "Alfredo's in the hospital, so I thought I'd come over and tell you myself."

"I heard about Alfredo. You really think they might shoot my horses?"

"I don't know. I just wanted to warn you, Mrs. Mesko. Some of your horses can be seen from the road. They make easy targets."

"Have you reported this?"

Ben said he had.

"Any idea who did it?"

Ben shook his head. He wasn't about to say George Trilby or Richie Lewis. "Deputy Metcalf said it might be a redneck, somebody practicing with a new rifle."

"In the dark?" Mrs. Mesko was frowning.

"They used a nightscope."

Mrs. Mesko took a deep breath and then said, "I'll move my horses into the back pastures."

"That might be a good idea," said Ben. "And would you ask your people to keep an eye open for anyone with a rifle?"

Mrs. Mesko nodded.

As Ben was turning to leave, she said, "Thank you, young man," with the slightest hint of warmth in her voice.

Sandy's mother dropped her off about three-fifteen, another girl having taken over the kiddie pool at Coto de Caza at three.

Ben held her fiercely for a long time, and she held him. He wanted to say, "I feel so alone," but decided not to. Why, he didn't know. He should be able to tell Sandy anything.

"I'll be all right tomorrow," he said. Better tomorrow but not all right, he knew. Days, maybe months, would pass before he'd be "all right" because of The Sisters.

Breaking away, he splashed cold water on his face. Why was it that he always got weepy around someone he knew? Alfredo? Sandy? Why was that? With his rear end hard against the sink, he cleared his throat, asking, "Who'd you tell I was going to be out here alone?"

Sandy frowned. "Jeez, I can't remember. That was two months ago when you first told me they were going. Why?"

"The deputy sheriff asked me who knew my folks had gone away. You didn't tell Julie Trilby, did you?"

"*What?*" Sandy's voice rose; her frown got wider. "You know I don't talk to her. I don't ever talk to her."

"Okay, okay," he said, knowing the two of them didn't get along.

"Why Julie Trilby?"

"That problem with her father's property."

"You think Trilby shot them?"

"I don't know what to think. The deputy said whoever

did it used a rifle with a night telescope like they used in Vietnam. Mrs. Mesko asked about Satan people."

Sandy said, worried, "You in danger here?"

Ben said, "I don't think I am, but the rest of the animals may be."

"I can ask Daddy to come over and spend the night with you. He volunteered to help this morning."

"No, no," Ben said instantly. A nice enough guy, Mr. Gilmore was not someone he'd want with him against a shooter. Luis, Rafael, Hudson, yes. Mr. Gilmore was an indoor man. He raised orchids and was a champion bridge player. The horses belonged to Sandy and her mother. "Hudson's here. Rafael, Luis." She knew them.

She was standing by the sink with her arms folded. "I still think your parents were lousy to leave all this in your lap."

"How could they know, Sandy? How could they know Alfredo would be in an accident? How could they know someone would turn cats out, shoot them?"

"Guess you're right," said Sandy, sighing.

She didn't like Ben's mother all that much, a subject they elected not to discuss at any length.

"Chances are it won't happen again. Last night might have been a fluke," Ben said.

Sandy said she hoped that was true and then said, "I'll come over tomorrow night, boost your morale."

He didn't discourage that idea. His morale needed boosting.

"I'll get Luis, and we'll take you home. We're headed for El Toro to pick up some bamboo fencing, try to see Alfredo . . ."

A moment later the CAT WAGN was rolling toward

the Gilmores', Sandy squeezed in between Luis and Ben, Rachel in the back end.

"Five minutes," the nurse said to Ben and Luis.

Alfredo was still hooked up to tubes. His head was bandaged, and his face was light gray rather than its usual brown. His eyes were closed. He looked bad.

Ben and Luis had decided not to tell him about the shooter, about the cats being turned out, about Daisy and Helen dead.

Ben held his hard hand and said, in not much more than a whisper, "Everything's fine, Alfredo. You just get well."

Alfredo opened his eyes, licked his lips, and nodded.

Ben said that they'd look after Graciela and the children.

Alfredo said thanks and closed his eyes again. He was still in critical condition.

Ben and Luis tiptoed out and went to Builders Emporium, across from the freeway, to buy the bamboo fencing.

Luis said he'd bring Graciela to the hospital that night while Rafael watched the kids.

Feeding Time

Ben always looked forward to the late afternoon "white bucket" hour, between five and six in the summer, earlier in the winter; the crackling of big cat electricity in the air.

After cleaver work by Rafael, the five-gallon white plastic buckets were loaded with about ten pounds each of red muscle meat or whole defeathered chickens, sometimes whole turkeys, larded with vitamins.

Premeal roars echoed throughout the preserve, cats waiting all day to be fed on their plywood square plates. There were quick fights, canines raking beige coats but doing no damage; snarls, machine-gunned tumult if any but the meekest thought its plate would be usurped by another.

Ben was on the preserve payroll for a hundred a week, and feeding the big cats daily was part of the work. Soon he joined Luis and Rafael in the rounds, white buckets in hand.

He was back at the house by six, and a few minutes later the phone rang.

"We know the rifle, Ben. Sniper type," Harry Metcalf said.

Sniper.

Just the word was threatening. Sniper.

Ben said, "You sure?"

"The lab identified it as a Remington 700, four grooves, right-hand twist. I looked it up. There's a military version fitted with a Redfield variable power telescopic sight, but that's not what this guy was using last night. He had to have a starscope. Now, to find out who he is? Where he got it?"

"Sniper," Ben repeated, feeling a sudden icy fright, though full darkness was still three hours away. Trilby with a rifle? Richie with a rifle?

"That's right," said the deputy. "I called the bureau to see . . ."

"The bureau?"

"The FBI . . . to see if they had any report from the military on a stolen starscope. They had one. Someone swiped it from the Navy's SEAL unit down on Coronado Island about six months ago."

Ben knew what SEALs were: Navy air, sea, and land commandos, guys who did underwater demolition, para-chuted from low-flying planes. They'd been in Vietnam.

"I've been thinking about it off and on all day," Ben said. "First he cuts the gate alarm system, so he knows something about electronics. Then he comes down on the road, goes right by Dmitri—knows enough to do that—and opens Number Three first, then Number Two, runs back up the road, up the hill, and waits for the cats to come out, planning to shoot them from up there. But they mill around and go in the opposite direction when the peacocks begin to yell. So he goes along the road and waits for the cats to get into the clear. The only cats that go into the clear are Helen and Daisy. That's why they died."

Harry Metcalf said, "Okay, why did he turn them out? He could have shot all of them from the road."

"I guess he wanted to rattle us. He did that, all right."

"Rattle you is as good a guess as any. Another subject. I talked to George Trilby this afternoon. He's got four rifles. I'll find a way to take a look at them. See if he has a Remington 700."

"That's a lot, four, isn't it?"

"Some hunters have ten."

"Ten?" Ben repeated.

"Don't worry about the number," said Metcalf. "They only shoot one at a time."

"Did you get that bamboo fencing?"

"We'll get it Friday. They said they'd have it today, but it hadn't come from the warehouse."

There were three nights until Friday. Three dark nights, the sliver of moon just beginning to fatten and brighten. "How about the other side?" the deputy asked.

Those were compounds on the east side, facing the Lewis property. "They'll have to be exposed until we get bamboo up over there."

"Tell you what, just until Friday go out and buy some of that cheap plastic drop cloth from a paint store, the opaque kind, and lash it to the fencing on that side. I think it's only four bucks a roll."

"Why didn't I think of that?"

"You would have tomorrow."

Ben shook his head in dismay. Alfredo would have thought of it instantly. "Should we keep a watch up on the road tonight?"

"I don't think so, if you've shifted those cats and drape those other compounds. Besides, I'm not sure I want you or anyone else up there. I don't need a homicide. See if you can get that bamboo earlier than Friday."

"Okay."

"Good luck," Metcalf said, and hung up.

Ben said to Rachel, "Come on." There was a Standard Brands near El Toro as well as several hardware stores.

Rachel bounded out of the house and into the CAT WAGN, leaping up between Ben and Luis, looking, looking. Cheetahs have a habit of watching, at home or on the road, watching everything, eyes shifting, narrowing. At home Rachel often sat by the windows and looked out at the big cats for hours. She was deathly afraid of them and had her own smaller fenced-in run at the side of the house.

Ben said to Luis as they rode along, "Trilby has four rifles."

Luis said, "That doesn't mean he shot the cats."

"But he has the rifles to do it, Deputy Metcalf said."

"He's not the type, Ben," said Luis, who had shopped at the country store until Trilby found out he worked for the Jepsons. Neither Ben nor his parents, even Graciela, had been able to shop at Trilby's. They all had to go into El Toro. Six years' worth of anger from Trilby.

Ben looked over. "How do you know that?"

"I just guess it."

They bought the plastic sheeting and padlocks, then hurried back home. By the time they returned to the canyon it was twilight, and the cats were in their usual vespers mood. There was a lot of grooming of heads and necks going on, places where the cats couldn't alone reach with their prickly tongues. Sometimes the sprucing-up took half an hour. The cats in compounds facing the lake were down on their bellies watching the ducks shuttle around.

Nice time of night, usually.

Ben, Luis, and Rafael began draping the bottoms of the east compounds, shielding them from the eyes and barrel of the shooter. They were talking about Alfredo, how he was improving.

Jilly Coombes arrived, and Ben said, "Grab this roll, Jilly."

With his flaming red hair and fair skin, stocky Jilly always looked red-faced, as though he'd just exercised, whether he had or not. Jilly and his mother swore they could get a sunburn under a reading lamp. He had an oval face and a mouthful of braces.

"That guy shoot any more today?" he asked.

"No," said Ben.

"Who do you think did it?" Jilly asked, holding up the doubled sheeting while Rafael and Luis tied it to the fence.

"We don't know," said Ben tiredly. "Deputy Metcalf is working on it." He was tired of answering "Who did it?"

"You got the sheriffs on it?" Jilly asked.

"Yeah," said Ben.

There wasn't enough drop cloth to cover all the fencing on that side, so Ben decided to leave open a ten-foot space in the center compound, Number Eleven, where Rocky was quartered. The cat hut, pushed up against the fence, took up about nine feet of that open space, so there was a gap of only a foot. He gave a set of keys to Luis and sent Rafael off on the mission of padlocking every compound. His father and Alfredo would have done it, he was sure.

On the way back to the house, Jilly and Ben stopped

by Hudson's Airstream. Seated in a canvas chair, reading a veterinary textbook, the Kenyan rose and, speaking in his soft British-Swahili accent, asked what he could do.

"Not anything, really," Ben replied.

"Would you like me to keep watch tonight? Up on the road?"

"The deputy sheriff said he thought we'd be okay if we locked everything, took the cats out of the exposed front compounds, and draped plastic sheeting on the back fences. He doesn't want humans shot."

Hudson said, "I do have some experience."

The London-educated vet, with his crinkly gray hair and trimmed gray beard, didn't look like a revolutionary now. He looked more like a gentle United Nations diplomat. Only the morning coat was missing.

"Thank you, but we'll see what happens tonight," Ben said.

"Have you heard from your father?"

"Nothing."

"I warned him. Poaching is a well-organized business over there, and they don't want interference. Several years ago the wardens caught a man who was responsible for four thousand zebra skins. Just one man."

"My dad's careful," Ben said.

"Sometimes careful is not enough," said the Kenyan. "The people who set the snares are lawless."

"I think he knows that."

"A poacher sets his rings of steel along paths to the water, and the loops catch a neck or leg. The harder the animal struggles to escape, the deeper goes the snare. They are brutal. I don't blame your father for wanting to write about them."

"Are they white men?"

"Some. But mostly are villagers. Many believe they have the right to kill. There is a Swahili phrase, *nyama ya mungu*. It means '*meat of God.*' They do not think they are doing wrong. They are very dangerous to outsiders."

Ben said his parents knew that and went off toward the house, not wanting to hear those dire words from Hudson Odinga.

Still nothing on the answering machine from East Africa, and Ben decided to call the Serengeti about 10:00 P.M. California time, early morning over there.

Jilly had brought four Big Macs, and Ben put them into the microwave while telling Jilly everything that had happened since the peacocks screamed.

Jilly had a nervous foot, his right one, and it tapped constantly whenever he was sitting still.

Ben had gotten used to it. This night was an exception. Ben said, "Jilly, sit on your foot."

"What do you mean?" he asked, mouth jammed with Big Mac.

"Put it under your leg."

Ben was jumpy, jittery.

Jilly nodded and took care of his foot. "I figure Richie Lewis did it," he said, chewing away.

"Why do you think so?" Ben asked, in an annoyed voice.

"What other ass-face out here would do it?" Jilly had a colorful way of speaking. His parents often used the old threat—washing his mouth out with laundry soap.

"Trilby," Ben said, almost angrily.

"Nah," Jilly said. "He's a human mouse." Jilly agreed with Luis Vargas.

"Deputy Metcalf said Trilby admitted he's got four rifles."

"So what? My oldest brother has two. Just because someone owns a rifle doesn't mean he's shooting lions."

"Trilby's got a reason. That land he owns."

"I still think it's Richie," Jilly said, echoing Luis again.

Jilly had his own personal reason. Last year, Richie and Jilly had both gone for the same parking space at the mini-mall at Trabuco village. Richie got out of his pickup and grabbed Jilly by the collar. Jilly had been threatening to "get" Richie ever since. Jilly was full of smoke a lot of times.

Jilly had already eaten his other Big Mac and got up to put some apple turnovers in the micro. He said, "What we ought to do is get masks and go wait in The Cootie parking lot for him to come out, then beat the livin' crap outta him."

"Outta who?" Ben asked.

"Richie Lewis," Jilly said, without batting an eye. "The two of us together weigh almost two-seventy, and he's at about two-forty, outta shape."

That was a typical Jilly idea, Ben thought. He said, "Jilly, we're not going to beat anybody up."

They'd done a lot of crazy things together, but putting on masks and jumping Richie in a beer joint parking lot wasn't going to be one of them, Ben thought. Though they were best friends, sometimes Jilly had weird ideas.

A few minutes later, Jilly said, "I know your folks don't believe in guns."

"No, they don't," Ben said.

"You want me to go home and get my pop's .38? He keeps it under the bed but won't miss it till this is all over. He keeps it loaded."

Ben said, "Thanks, Jilly. I'll do fine without it."

Jilly went home after nine, though Ben was tempted to ask him to stay. It was now completely dark down in the canyon, and he had an uneasy feeling. Late at night it was usually quiet in the preserve. A few cars would speed along the hardtop; an occasional aircraft would whine overhead. Now and then, a cat would break the silence with a half-hearted roar. In the distance, coyotes would howl. Often, the Mexicans would have Tijuana music on their radios. But by midnight all would be relatively quiet and mysterious, only the tigers, leopards, and jaguars awake.

A Creaking

Rachel was now perched on the ottoman by the picture window, scanning the dim road in front of the cottage and the compounds across the way, watching the doves that winged into the cottonwoods to spend the night. The ottoman was her favorite observation post.

There were pole lights by the parking area for the house; a wall fixture just outside the front door; another higher one that beamed down on the porch decking. So there was some scanty illumination out there. But they'd always turned all lights off on going to bed, and the sniper didn't need light with that starscope.

Ben rubbed Rachel's head, and she twisted around to look at him. Their eyes were almost level. A vain cat, she knew her own black-spotted beauty. The cheetah's face, with the horseshoe lines running from the eyes to the corners of the mouth, was the most distinctive of all cats. Last time they'd weighed her she was a few ounces over ninety pounds. Fastest animal alive, she could accelerate to forty-five miles per hour in two seconds, then go up to seventy-five at full speed. Rachel had her own supersized "cat" door to go to her run alongside the house. She was a fastidious animal, toilet-trained long ago, a fine house cat.

He said to her, "Time for my walk."

Usually somewhere between eight and ten, one of the Jepsons, or all of them, took an after-dinner "all's well" inspection walk around the compounds. Winter, spring, summer, fall. While making the rounds, they talked to the cats who came to the fences, wanting human contact. They went into one or another compound to check on an animal that was ill. Cats were just as susceptible to colds, disease, or even cancer, as humans.

His father and mother often held hands on these walks, as if they were young lovers. On moonlit nights they would stop by the lake for a while, sitting quietly and counting blessings for being able to live day and night among the animals they loved. Sometimes Ben would sit with them, listen to their subdued talk, ask a question. Those were the good times.

The lions reminded Ben of old people, lazy old people; the tigers and jaguars were like the secretive Mafia, the hitmen. He knew each of the ninety-two cats by name, recognizing them by a floppy ear or bowlegs or a scar. No, ninety now.

On the infrequent rainy nights, the Jepsons put on slickers and boots, sloshing around the compound pathways, visiting the tigers, who loved the raw, cold weather, the downpours. Lions were not to be seen, hating mud and dampness. During winter, the lions usually went to bed early, entering their huts at twilight, while the tigers stayed up much later. During cold weather heat lamps were always provided for the older cats.

At nine o'clock, Ben was making the night walk alone, feeling insecure as he went along. Seeing their eyes shine in the darkness, he was suddenly aware that the cats' safety was completely in his hands. He hadn't thought about that all day. Not in those terms.

Going down the east row of compounds, pausing to say hello to the cats in Number Seven, calling to them by name, he put the back of his hand against the chain-link to be licked, noting the new padlock on the gate. He tugged at it.

In Number Eight, Pasha lion had five lionesses in his harem, all on birth control, but one of them, poor Nellie, was dying of bone cancer, not responding to chemotherapy. She was losing her coat, her beauty. Her eyes said she wanted to go, peacefully.

Ben went in and sat down beside her, rubbing her back. "You feel any better tonight?"

She looked up at him, eyes dull.

"No, you don't."

Then she looked away, into the night.

Ben stroked her silently for about five minutes, then went out of the compound.

In some ways, the cats *were* like humans, tending to be restless when high winds cut through the canyon, stirring dust devils. In bright moonlight, the tigers paced and prowled, as did the jaguars. The leopards and cougars always seemed to be awake but stayed in the shadows.

Compound Eleven

Ben went into Compound Eleven where Rocky was residing alone for the time being, saying hello to his lion, hugging him, telling him everything was going to be okay. Stay mellow, Rocky boy.

Ben had placed Chico and Mikey in Number Nine, along with dotty old Henry, just to play it safe. Rocky might not have harmed them, but with all the activity, cats being shifted around, a feeling of tension in the preserve, better not to take the chance.

Lately, Rocky had developed a bad case of possessiveness, somewhat like human jealousy but a lot more dangerous. There was no known cure for it, but Ben wasn't about to give up on his favorite lion.

Sandy had been involved in the onset. About four months before the Jepsons flew off to Africa, she'd ridden Dolly, her sorrel mare, up to the preserve in the late afternoon, tying her just inside the main gate, well away from the compounds. She went down to the house and, finding Mrs. Jepson inside, asked for Ben.

Dorothy said, "Oh, hi, Sandy. He's on his walk with Rocky. It's after four."

That meant along the Naranja, or if he'd finished the river walk, he'd likely be by the lake.

"I'll find him," said Sandy, trudging off toward the lake, passing the animal compounds. Ben had long ago introduced her to the "safe" cats like Helen and Jessica and Rocky, taking her inside the chain-link fencing, letting her hug them. She'd met panthers and cougars and Bengal tigers as well as lions, experiencing the same thrill that Ben had experienced when he was eight.

As she went by Number Fourteen on her left, home of four Bengals, she spotted Ben and Rocky at the picnic table down by the lake. Ben was on a bench and the lion was by his side, on all fours.

A few ducks were enjoying the water, fluttering and sailing about, and Rocky's big head was pointed in their direction when Sandy called out, "I knew exactly where to find you."

Suddenly the head swerved around, Rocky rising up in a blur, roaring, then charging, as Ben yelled, "No! No! No!"

Rocky got to within ten feet of Sandy, rearing up on his hind legs, claws out, canines bared, the roar a torrent of sound.

Sandy screamed, too terrified to even run.

Ben was shocked. Rocky had always been so friendly toward Sandy.

Ben shouted, "No, Rocky! No!" But he knew better than to make a move toward the lion. It was always best to stay still; to freeze. Shout and freeze, criss-crossing arms.

The lion turned toward Ben again, beginning to pace

back and forth in front of his father-mother, acting as if to protect him, still glaring at Sandy, the intruder, making deep chest threats, tail whipping.

Ben could feel the jealous rage in Rocky. Something had snapped up in that beautiful head without warning.

Ben's dad was by the bulldozer shed when he heard the scream and came on the double toward the lake. Any scream in the preserve brought immediate help, and Peter Jepson, as he ran up, was yelling, "No, no! Leave it, Rocky! Leave it!" Though they often worked, they were not magic words.

Rocky instantly changed his target from Sandy, who had collapsed, to Ben's dad. The lion seemed to have gone berserk.

Then Alfredo came running up, and Rocky charged him, too, making that terrifying chest rumble.

Ben was speechless, staying by the picnic bench, trying to remember everything he'd ever been told about a charging big cat. But this was different from other stand-offs with the animals.

After each charge, the lion returned to Ben, pacing back and forth, guarding, bodily pushing him away from the three humans.

"Get out of sight, Ben," the elder Jepson yelled. "Go to the lake house."

Slowly, Ben began to work his way to the cottage, mainly used for parties, at the edge of the lake, moving a foot or so at a time, Rocky rumbling, eyes afire with anger.

Had he gone insane?

Ben didn't know. He only knew he was frightened of this cat for the first time in his life.

Finally, his rear end made contact with the porch rail

and he slipped inside, hearing his dad begin a dialogue with Rocky, using a gentle, soothing voice.

As Ben stood behind the door, breathing as though he'd just run ten miles, drenched in sweat, he heard the rumble subsiding.

Then after a while, he heard his dad saying, in a normal voice, "Here we go, young man," and knew that Rocky was being led away.

He waited until he thought they were out of sight; then he went out to Sandy, who was still sitting on the ground. Her head was down on her wrists, which were on her knees.

He lifted her up and held her, telling her it was all over. Color slowly came back into her face. She asked what had happened.

Ben said he didn't know.

He soon drove her home. They didn't talk much on the way.

Ben's dad knew what had happened.

"I tried to warn you. Rocky suddenly got himself a big, bad case of possessiveness today, and it's not going away. He thinks he has to protect you against people, other cats, anything that might harm you."

"Why?" Ben asked. Sandy harm him? Rocky had flipped!

"Single-minded possessiveness that dates back to cubhood. You knew I was worried about it. Now I don't want you going into that compound, ever. He'll kill the other cats. You want to walk him, let him come outside. When you do walk him, avoid everyone else. Don't go near anyone. He'll charge. Your relationship with Rocky has changed, Ben. Understand it!"

Ben found that hard to believe and went outside, picking up a lead off the porch rail, going to Rocky's compound, calling out to his lion at the gate.

Rocky trotted over, and Ben swung the gate open, looping the lead around Rocky's neck, noticing at the same time that the other lions stayed against the far fence. Were they afraid? Maybe the other lions knew it, too. Maybe they knew Rocky would attack them if Ben entered. Maybe his dad was right.

They walked along the Naranja for almost a quarter of a mile toward the Carpenters' trailer park as if nothing had happened that day, Rocky as gentle as ever.

In the evening, he called Sandy to say he couldn't explain it aside from jealousy.

"I don't want that to ever happen again," said Sandy. "I'm still shaky. Did you see the way he was looking at me?"

"I saw."

"You better tell him I don't want to compete. I'll do that with two-legged females but not with him. Ben, he was ready to kill me. Don't you realize that?"

"Come on, Sandy. He was just making a lot of noise."

"Yeah, pacing back and forth . . ."

"You've seen them do that before."

"But not with me in mind. From now on, I'm staying far away from Rocky."

"Maybe he'll change."

"I'm not taking the chance."

Four months had passed, many visits to the preserve, but not once had Sandy gone near Rocky's compound.

The Purring Cats

Ben stayed with Rocky a few minutes longer, digging deep into his mane, then moved on.

The two jaguars, General Pico and Iris, natives of Argentina, were in Number Twelve. Most ferocious of all the cats, the only ones known to do battle with eight-foot alligators, the General and Iris were left to themselves and seemed to prefer it that way.

Next door were the leopards. He entered their compound, careful not to present his back to Dora, a black animal with pale hypnotic eyes. She'd leap from behind. Some people called the black ones panthers, but they were really leopards, their spots showing through in bright sunlight. The leopards were always hiding in the trees, leaves and branches providing cover. Isabel, his favorite, came off a limb, and he knelt down in the sand to kiss and caress her, wishing he could shelter them all in the house.

In Number Fourteen were the cougars, America's only native lion. They were also called pumas, catamounts, panthers, and mountain lions. They could outjump tigers and leopards, dropping unerringly from sixty feet up in a tree to a deer's back. Hunters and ranchers having a vendetta against them, the safest place for cougars now was in captivity. Entering the compound, he rubbed Max's russet head, and then gave attention to Gertrude when she came purring up. The fur of a cougar was like down. He spent about five minutes inside Number Fourteen, then continued his walk.

On the west side, by the lake, he was startled by a voice coming out of the darkness. "It's me, Hudson," the voice said.

He aimed the flashlight toward the sound and saw the tall Kenyan standing in the high grass at the point where The Sisters had been shot.

Ben walked over.

"Good evening, Benjamin," Hudson said, formally. He never used Ben.

"You startled me."

Odinga said, "I needed some air and thought I'd come out and take another look around. Think I'll go up and walk along the road."

"Watch out," Ben said, thinking of Metcalf's warning.

The Kenyan nodded. "I do have experience in this."

"Just the same, be careful. The sheriff told me he's an expert marksman. He's using a nightscope."

"What warned you this morning?"

"The peacocks," Ben said.

Hudson nodded. "In the forest we were always warned of the enemy by the monkeys and birds."

Saying good night, he faded away into the darkness.

Ben watched as he vanished, thinking about what Jilly had said—borrowing his father's .38. There were no firearms at Los Coyotes, but there were the gas-cartridge dart guns. They could cripple, even kill. He stood a moment, then went over to the little hospital, opened it, and got one of the loaded dart Lugers out of a drawer.

Last, he stopped by Dimmy. The Siberian was wide awake. Ben couldn't remember when the tiger hadn't been awake at night. He slept by day. Dimmy came to the fence when called, but Ben avoided direct eye contact. Tigers seldom made eye contact unless they were committed to battle. Ben had seen that happen only once and hoped never to see it again: Dimmy and his brother, Sergei. A fight for dominance. The chilling sounds of the two animals had started in their bowels, and Ben held his breath. Their chests had been bellows. Dimmy won, and the brothers were separated forever, even kept out of each other's sight. Sergei had never fully recovered from his wounds. Dmitri was that savage.

Tigers were always different, mysterious animals, even as cubs. Ben could pick up any lion cub and cuddle it. Not so with tigers. Screaming, they let it be known they wanted all four feet on the ground. Lion cubs loved to play, but tiger cubs wanted combat. By a year old, they couldn't be controlled in play, Ben had learned. Ears flattened back, eyes almost glazed, they went into a fighting mode. As adults, the lazy lion heart beat at forty per minute while the resting tiger beat at sixty-four. There was a big difference.

> *Tyger! Tyger! burning bright*
> *In the forests of the night,*
> *What immortal hand or eye*
> *Could frame thy fearful symmetry?*

His father was fond of quoting William Blake's poem, and he'd told Ben about an ancient Islamabad legend that if one touched a ferocious tiger, an invisible magic sword would leap into the hand and the holder would be invincible. Someday Ben intended to go inside Number One, touch the Siberian, come out alive, holding the magic sword, and use it to slay Richie Lewis.

But he said good night to Dimmy without looking at him and went on into the house, knowing that sleep might be difficult.

The voice of the Chief Park Warden wavered over the thousands of miles: "We haven't been able to contact them and, quite frankly, I'm a bit concerned. Your father is very experienced in the bush, I realize, but he's involved in a rather risky undertaking. Poachers place as little value on human life as they do on animal life."

"How often did you try yesterday?" Ben asked, again wondering why his parents weren't monitoring the calls.

"Ten minutes at a crack, on the hour."

"And just silence back from them?"

"I'm afraid so. We're sending an aircraft toward Kirawira this afternoon to look for them. Meanwhile, we'll keep trying by radio. If we do contact them, what message do you want to give?"

Ben thought a moment. Someone else telling them The Sisters had been shot by a sniper, that Alfredo was in the hospital wasn't the way to do it. He said, "Just please have them call me as soon as possible."

"All right, then," said the warden, "and I'll keep you posted on whatever happens here."

Sniper. The picture in his mind wouldn't go away no matter how hard he tried: someone hidden by darkness carefully aiming his rifle, sighting through the scope, waiting until the exact moment to squeeze the trigger.

Turning off all the lights, he went out to the porch again to look and listen. Except for the hum of night bugs and frogs down by the lake, Los Coyotes was enclosed in thick, black silence.

The county road was hidden from his view by the leafy cottonwoods and oaks, but he still looked up there, wondering if the sniper was aiming that starscope down toward the compounds. Staying out there about twenty minutes, listening and looking, tense in every muscle, he went back inside, locked the door, and went on to his bedroom, followed by the padding Rachel.

Placing the dart gun on the table beside his bed, he sprawled on his back, trying to make his ears as sensitive as those of the cats.

Fear. He knew well what physical fear was—facing an angry cat, for instance. But this was a sinister fear he'd never faced before.

He now had a mental picture of the sniper. He was big, shaggy. He had a loose mouth. Luis and Jilly had planted something in Ben's head. The sniper was Richie Lewis.

Soon, Rachel was snoring at the foot of the bed, making it impossible for him to hear anything else. He got up on his knees, hitting her with a pillow, yelling for her to stop. She looked up, surprised by the attack.

Nerves. He'd gotten jitters before a Pony League

game, but after the second or third hike they were always behind him.

He'd never been so edgy in his life.

He'd drift off, then awaken with a start.

About two o'clock, he awakened, hearing a creaking in the direction of the front door. The old boards of the house often creaked in dry weather, but this seemed steady, and he thought, *He's inside.*

Lifting the dart gun off the table, he slipped out of bed, moving quickly toward the living room. The creaking continued.

Heart pounding as it had in the early morning, he yelled "Freeze!" in his best *Miami Vice* fashion, trying to make himself sound adult, then suddenly realized the creaking was outside.

Going over to the window, he expected to see a form on the porch. The creaking was louder than ever now, and he became aware that a light wind had sprung up.

They'd built the porch around a tree, and the wooden collar was in contact with it. Remembering now that wind always made the tree creak against the collar, Ben's heart-beats began to calm down.

"Jerk," he said to himself, heading to his room.

Back in bed, hearing the creaking, he rolled and tossed for what must have been another two hours, more than ever resenting his parents' trip to the Serengeti. They didn't need the money! They did those things for prestige more than anything else. Ego. The least they could do is call me, he thought. It was now eleven days since they'd flown off. Not one single call to say, "How ya' doin', pal?"

SECOND DAY

Rachel

Eyes stinging, mouth dry, Ben woke up after daylight feeling weary. Debating on whether or not to try for more sleep, he stayed still, then came out of bed in stages: yawning, flexing shoulders, sitting on the edge of the bed, dangling feet. Looking around the room, he couldn't see Rachel. But she often went out to her run at daybreak to watch as the morning arrived.

Still groggy, he went to the john, washing his face, brushing his teeth, then decided to take a cold shower and try to wake up. That helped.

But it was a full ten minutes before he was pouring a glass of guava juice, getting English muffins out of the freezer. At the sink, he suddenly turned around. *That's odd*, he thought. Rachel usually came in through her cat door when she heard someone in the kitchen.

Going quickly to the window, he looked down into the run. Lying on her side, the cheetah appeared to be asleep. She never slept in the early morning. She was always up, observing the new day, watching, listening.

With a sick feeling, Ben ran out of the house and around to the side-run gate, pulling it open. Even from the gate, he could see blood staining the sand around Rachel, not dried or crusted as yet. She hadn't been dead long.

He didn't cry this time, not at this moment, just sat down beside her, rubbing her, his face as blank as white marble. She looked as though she was sound asleep, beautiful even in death. The bullet hit her, and she just fell over. In place, he thought. Didn't make a move, he thought. Bull's-eye again. Sniperscope again. Same man. Richie Lewis?

After a while, he got up and walked slowly up to Alfredo's mobile home, feeling as old as the canyon floor. Graciela let him in.

"He got Rachel," Ben said, without emotion, without expression.

"Oh, no," said Graciela.

"After dawn, I think. That's when she usually goes out."

"In the run?"

Ben nodded, face still a blank.

Graciela came over, putting her arms around Ben. Rachel was the only cat she could, or would, pet. She'd often come up to the house just to visit Rachel, bringing the children. She loved the cheetah, as they all did.

After telling Luis, Ben knocked on Hudson's door, asking him to recover the bullet.

On the way back to the house, he broke down and sobbed, clinging to the chain-link of Number Twenty-eight, his finger joints white, his back shuddering. Then, sucking in breath and blowing out, he plodded on.

He tried to eat breakfast but had no appetite, knowing

Rachel was down in the sand twenty feet away. Coffee was all he could handle. He saw Hudson's head bobbing around out there.

Luis came to the house in a little while, carrying a tarp, and they went out to the run, rolled Rachel into it, backed the cat wagon up to the gate, and took her out by the oak where The Sisters were buried, using the backhoe to dig another hole.

Then they went to her run, looking up toward the road. There was a space between the trees that made it easy to draw a bead on the cheetah. So easy. It was his fault, Ben thought. He'd never considered Rachel a target.

Behind the glass wall, he could see his mother's lips moving. "You should have kept her inside, Ben! Use your head!"

Back in the house, he called Deputy Metcalf, telling him another cat had been killed.

"In a compound?"

"No, our cheetah, Rachel, in her run on the south side of the house."

Metcalf groaned. "What is it with this guy? He must be nuts. I find him, he's damn well gonna serve some time. I'll come by after a while to get the bullet. Then I want to go and talk to Richie Lewis."

Ben was all for that. He hung up and wept until his ribs hurt.

Three dead. When would it stop?

One of the chores on the list Ben's dad had left for them was to weigh the cats, except Dmitri. Dimmy could await the return from Africa. A chart was kept on each cat, recording general health, and each was weighed annually.

Keep busy, Ben said to himself; *keep moving, do things. Weigh some cats. Try not to think of Rachel.* Luis and Rafael hauled the scale to unoccupied Number Five, setting it up in there, then got Jo-Jo out of Number Eight and walked him over, got the big Rhodesian in position, and Ben listed his weight on the chart at four hundred eighty-three pounds, a very big lion. Luis had him loosely on a lead. He seemed to be behaving himself this morning.

As Ben walked away from the scale, he tripped on a clump of grass, falling face down in the sand, still holding the chart board. Before he could push up and get away, Jo-Jo was on him, covering his body, canines closing over the back of his skull, Zacatecas straw spinning off.

Jo-Jo didn't try to crush the head that was between his canines, seeming content just to hold it like a large coconut. But Ben could feel the pressure of the fangs, smell the hot, sour breath that flowed around his face.

This had happened to his dad once, he remembered. He had told Ben, "I stayed still. Absolutely still."

So Ben told himself, "Stay still, absolutely still; don't move a muscle."

Luis was also advising, "Stay still, Ben; stay still."

"What do you think I'm doing?" he answered, nose in the sand.

Ben knew exactly how much Jo-Jo weighed, and every pound was crushing him. Enclosed by the animal's body, he could feel the heat of his belly, the slow, rhythmic breathing, even the powerful heartbeat.

He heard Luis saying, "Get off, Jo-Jo, get off him! Quit playing games!"

Jo-Jo was playing Rocky's game of possession, and Ben

well knew that game. The cats played possession with bowling balls and other sturdy toys, with other objects of any description—clothing, cameras, a dishpan. Anything. But seldom humans.

Now, as Luis came closer, saying, "Come on, dammit, get off him, Jo-Jo," the lion growled, and the growl turned into the machine-gunning "Uh-huh, uh-huh," deep down in his chest.

Ben also knew what that meant: *"He's mine, he's mine, he's mine!"*

Ben heard Luis telling Rafael, in Spanish, "Get the fire extinguishers," then saying to Ben, "Keep calm, keep calm . . ."

Ben's muffled reply was, "What do you think I'm trying to do?"

Looking sideways, he could see Luis's boots. They were seven or eight feet away. Luis kept talking to Ben, encouraging him, while waiting for Rafael to return. He'd given up talking to Jo-Jo.

Then: "Okay, Ben, we're going to try and smoke him."

Ben heard Luis shouting, "Leave it, leave it, Jo-Jo," and then heard the hollow *whoosh* come out of the black cone; felt the coldness of the gas as it enveloped the lion.

Jaws tightening, the guttural growls became louder. Jo-Jo wasn't about to give up. Ben felt his head being lifted, as if he might be dragged across the sand by the skull. He yelled, "Stop it!" To Luis, not to Jo-Jo. The gas cut off, and he felt his head being lowered again, growls muting. He tried to take deep breaths and slow his heart, thinking it might pound out of his body.

He'd now been within Jo-Jo's grasp for twenty minutes and wondered how long he could last. Would Jo-Jo tire of this game? At least he hadn't bitten down with those saw-tooth jaws yet. Some reasoning had to be within that huge head.

Luis said, "We'll try the tin."

"The tin" was a thin sheet of corrugated iron, some-times used on misbehaving cats, waved in front of their faces, making a rippling noise that usually frightened the animals.

Thinking that the tin, with its rippling noise, would only annoy Jo-Jo, Ben squeezed out, "Try the plywood."

"Okay," Luis said. "Hang on, it'll be a minute."

They had to go to the mechanical shed, where the plywood was stacked.

Hang on, stay still, Ben told himself. Trying to relax, he let every muscle sag.

Jo-Jo was like a huge, breathing beanbag.

The growling had stopped, and maybe the play session was over; maybe the human bowling ball was no longer of interest.

Suddenly, the growling began again, spikes of teeth pressing down on Ben's skull. Though the wounds were superficial, blood began to trickle down over his ears and forehead.

Just as suddenly the sheet of plywood, held on each side by Luis and Rafael, came hurtling at the big Rhodesian, and Ben was released as Jo-Jo sprang up and scrambled away.

Then Luis was there, saying, "You hokay, *señor?*" grin-ning widely. "That was quite a show you two put on," he said, trying to make light of it. "He scratched you!"

Ben said, "He bit me," rubbing his fingers over his forehead, seeing blood on them.

"Doesn't look bad to me," said Luis.

"Yeah, but I better get a tetanus." Mouths of the big cats were always loaded with bacteria.

He sat there a little longer, breathing deeply, Jo-Jo tied off about thirty feet away, looking over at him as if nothing had happened.

He finally got up, saying to Luis, "Put him back into his compound; then you better drive me to Emergency. All I need now is an infection."

Luis shrugged and went over to Jo-Jo.

Ben picked up the Zacatecas and wobbled down the sandy road toward home as if he were drunk.

Luis awakened Ben near two o'clock, saying, "The county man is here."

Up on his elbows, Ben asked, "What county man?"

"Animal Control."

"He's all we need today."

Four hours of exhausted, dreamless sleep after they got home from the emergency room had ended abruptly, and now it was just a matter of getting the cotton out of his head. The experience with Jo-Jo hadn't set in yet. It would, later, when he'd had time to think it over, remember the hot breath, the weight and warmth of that huge body.

Luis said, "He's going around on his own."

Ben got up, put his boots on, washed his face, and followed Luis out of the house.

"When did he get here?"

"About ten minutes ago. I was tempted to let you sleep."

"I'm okay," Ben said. What a joke!

Frank Coffey was an inspector for Animal Control and paid unannounced visits, checking on the freezer and food, checking for fence safety violations, making sure minimum-space requirements for the cats were being observed and sanitation requirements being met. Ben knew him.

He caught up with Coffey, a pot-gutted man in his early forties, outside Number Three. Though he wasn't required to wear a uniform, as an inspector, it always seemed to Ben he had one on: khaki pants, ankle-top boots, knit shirt. He'd sooner go without his boots than without his notebook, the Jepsons believed.

Ben said, yawning, "Hello, Mr. Coffey."

The inspector turned, saying curtly, "Where's your father?"

"They're both away," Ben said.

Before he could ask where, Ben added, "Not for long."

Coffey looked into the compound. "You got new straw in the dens?"

"Yes."

Thank God they'd raked the feces out of all the compounds on Monday, drying and bagging it for sale at an El Toro garden shop. People said it kept deer out of their gardens. Ben scoffed at that notion. Nonetheless, they got ten dollars a bag for it.

Coffey turned around. "Hear you had some trouble night before last."

It was obvious he didn't know about Rachel as yet. "Yes, we did."

Coffey nodded. "Sheriff's department is required to notify us of anything involving animals. I notice your father didn't call."

"He must have forgotten," Ben said.

"Who did it?" Coffey asked.

"The deputy said he thought it was some weirdo taking night target practice." *Don't involve the neighbors*, Ben thought.

Coffey nodded again and started walking.

"I hear he got inside the fences and turned some lions loose."

Following him up the pathway, Ben said, "That's correct, Mr. Coffey." Ben made himself be polite, fought to make himself be polite.

Coffey stopped. "I thought all your gates were locked up at night."

"They are now."

"Did the lions get outside the perimeter fencing?"

"No, sir, they did not."

"Maybe I should recommend you get security guards for these gates at night?"

"That isn't necessary, Mr. Coffey. We have the electronic system, and now the compound gates are padlocked."

Coffey nodded, and they started off again. At Number Five, he said, "Where are the animals that were in here?"

"They were visible from the road. We shifted them to the other row so they can't be seen from up there. We've ordered bamboo shielding for these three compounds. It'll be up day after tomorrow."

"Aren't you overcrowding over there?"

You miserable creep, Ben thought. *Just aching for an excuse, any excuse, to close us down.* "Temporarily. Give us thirty-six hours."

113

"You know there are space requirements, don't you? Your father does."

"We know that, but this is an emergency, Mr. Coffey. The sheriff's department recommended we do this."

Coffey said, "Well, they better be shifted back by Saturday."

"They will be, I promise." For their sakes, not yours! Ben was wild.

Frank Coffey hadn't come over just to inspect. He'd come over, probably called by Trilby or Richie Lewis, to see what kind of trouble he could cause. Plenty. They were necessary, these people who inspected restaurants, hospitals, animal parks. But they could cause trouble even when you were doing everything right. Pull out black books and find a dozen teeny things wrong. Threaten you, cite you. Even close you down.

"Bureaucratic little creeps," in his mother's nicer words. Well, why wasn't she here now, with her sharp tongue?

Coffey continued his "inspection," stopping by the meat chopping blocks where Rafael was wielding a cleaver, then sticking his head into the animal hospital, looking around inside and sniffing. He suddenly turned to ask, "Your father bury those lions on the property?"

"Yes."

"How deep?"

"Eight feet."

"He put lime on them?"

"Yes."

Coffey walked on down the line of compounds on the east side silently, stopping at each one, making a note twice. Ben glanced over his shoulder.

114

"Overcrowding," he'd written.

Ben and Luis followed him grimly.

At the parking lot, the Animal Control man said, "I'll see you Saturday."

"Fine."

They watched him drive off, Luis spitting into the sand. "*Cabrón*," he said. *He-goat*.

Ben was beginning to realize there was more to running the preserve than locking the gates and feeding the animals.

Deputy Metcalf called in the late afternoon and said he'd visited Richie and old Jack, saw some rifles, some trophies.

"Maybe I shouldn't be telling all this to a fifteen-year-old, but I'm interested in pinning a charge on Mr. Lewis and need any help you can give me, your father not being around. I looked at his record before I went over there. Assault four times. Drunken driving twice. Last month we answered a call from The Cootie and there was Richie, out in the parking lot, straddling a guy, rubbing his face in the dirt. He squirmed out of it, proving he was aggravated. Refresh my memory about the trouble between the Lewises and your dad."

Ben did.

"Okay," said Metcalf. "He's got three rifles, or at least he showed me three, but none were Remington 700's. He's also got half a dozen shooting trophies—Stroh's Orange County Shoot-Out Expert Marksman; Winchester 1983 Meet; Remington Arms Meet 1985, and others."

Ben now thought Jilly and Luis Vargas were probably

right. Richie was the one, not Trilby. He had to face facts, like them or not.

Metcalf continued, "I'll go after a search warrant. Take his place apart. That may rattle him, but what we need to do is catch him in the act. So I'd appreciate it if you'd ask everyone to keep an eye open. We'd really like to take his hide."

Second Night

Jilly got there first, a bag of McDonald's fries in his hand, and then Sandy came along on her bike with a pound of chicken salad and a long loaf of French bread she'd picked up in the afternoon. All Ben had to do was come up with forks and knives, margarine, and something to drink.

Ben told them about Rachel and Jo-Jo and then about the visit from the Animal Control guy. Nothing had gone right this day. Nothing.

Jilly brought up Richie Lewis again. He hadn't changed his mind. Richie was the one.

"Metcalf said he had sharpshooting trophies but not the right rifle," Ben said. Everything kept pointing toward Richie, dammit.

Jilly said, "He may be hiding that Remington."

"That's what Metcalf said," Ben acknowledged.

Sandy came out with the chicken salad and French bread, setting them next to Jilly's fries. "Said about who?"

"Richie Lewis," Jilly and Ben said, almost in unison.

"I've only seen him that once," she said. "That time

you pointed at him outside The Cootie. He looked like the 'Original Goon.' "

Jilly said, "He is the Original Goon."

Ben knew if his father had been there, he would have driven over to face Richie in two minutes. Alfredo the same.

Jilly said, "I had another idea to make him stop."

"What's that?" Ben asked.

"Well, we put on masks and . . ."

Ben broke in, "Jilly, I heard that crap last night."

"Let me finish," Jilly said. "We put on masks and get Richie outside The Cootie, put him in the back of the cat wagon, bring him here, and guess what . . .?"

"What?"

Jilly grinned. "Give him squirts he'll never forget. Back that wagon up to Dmitri's compound and open the door."

Ben said, "Jilly, you're insane."

"That's the most awful thing I've ever heard of," Sandy said. "Even for him. Let that tiger eat him?" She knew Dmitri.

Jilly said, "No! Just scare that big peckerneck, scare him so bad he'll never even look at another cat, big or little."

"And the next day he gets us arrested for kidnapping," Ben said.

"Naw. We wear masks and gloves and don't say a word to each other. We blindfold him until we get right up against Dimmy's gate. Nobody'll ever believe we backed him up against a tiger pen."

Ben shook his head. "Jilly, I'll give you A for originality but F for brains. We haul him in the cat wagon; we bring him here? And you think he wouldn't know who did it? He's a peckerneck, all right, but he's not that dumb."

"He couldn't prove who did it."

Sandy said, "He might have a heart attack just facing Dmitri."

Jilly grinned over. "That wouldn't be too bad, would it?"

Ben said, "I just have to think you're not serious."

Jilly kept on grinning. "Oh, but I am."

"Well, forget it," Ben said. But Jilly's idea did have some appeal, the more he thought of it: Richie looking into Dimmy's greenish eyes. Terror on Richie's face, that loose mouth drawn up tight for once. He sat there, fork poised over his plate, seeing that picture of Richie.

Then he broke out of his reverie with a start. "Forget it," he said again. "We're not doing it."

Jilly went home about eight-thirty, but Sandy stayed on, and they went inside and washed the dishes. The usual evening coolness had settled into the canyon after a three o'clock high of over a hundred.

Sandy asked, "You want to watch some TV or just talk?"

"I'm totally bushed," Ben said, yawning widely. "Out of it." As usual these days.

Sandy peered over at him with her brown eyes. "I could help you go to sleep."

"How?" he said.

"Oh, I have my ways." The eyes held both a secret and a promise.

He smiled at her and leaned over to tag her lips with a kiss, then tossed the dishtowel to the drainboard.

They went over to one of the huge sofas, with the tricolored swansdown throw from Mbala on it. He dropped his body into the deep softness with a sigh and closed his eyes, Sandy sinking down next to him, putting his head into her lap.

119

Her fingertips worked over his temples, under his jaw. "Relax," she said softly.

"Where'd you learn to do this?"

"From an East Indian concubine."

He didn't laugh. "What's that?"

"Look it up."

Eyes still closed, he said, "I've got no guts, Sandy, or I'd go over there tomorrow."

"Go where?"

"To Richie's and face him."

"You said there wasn't any proof."

"It figures it's him, Sandy. No one else. Everything points to Richie, and I'm still scared to death of him. I get something in the hollow of my throat when I even think about him. He's always had it in for us, and I think someone told him my parents were going away. I don't think he'd be doing it if my father were here."

Sandy was silent.

"I've avoided him all this time," Ben confessed. "If he came by on the road, I'd turn my head away. If I saw him gassing up at the Arco, I'd drive ten miles on further to the 76. If I saw his pickup outside the mini-mall, I wouldn't go in. I've run from him all this time, and he never even threatened me."

"I don't blame you for being scared of him. Just his looks would frighten most people," she said. "There are people all over this world who are afraid of other people."

Lifting his head off her lap, he said, "Why the hell can't I just work up the guts to go over there and say, 'Richie, stop killing our cats or you're a dead man.' My father would do it; Alfredo would do it."

Sandy thought about that for a moment and then said,

"Ben, you've got to have some proof or he'll laugh you away. He won't take it seriously."

Proof? Ben dropped his head back to her thighs. Whether he took it seriously or not wasn't the idea. The idea was going up to Richie without his knees turning to jelly.

"Hudson said he thought we should all go up there tonight and wait for him. But Deputy Metcalf already said that was a bad idea. Someone could get shot."

They were talking between long spaces of thoughtful silence.

Ben said, "Why is it that I'm not afraid of lions and tigers? I'm not even afraid to face Jo-Jo, even after what happened today, after what he did to me."

Again, there was a silence.

Fear was Dmitri. "Someday I'm going in with him to prove myself."

"With who?"

"With Dimmy. Touch him and I get a magic sword. I'd be invincible."

"Who told you that?"

"My dad. It's an old legend from Pakistan."

"You might know," said Sandy. "I think it has to do with the rites of manhood for both of you."

"What are the rites of manhood?"

"They date back to the cave people. Young warrior goes out to slay a grizzly bear with a big rock."

Fear was six-three, weighed two-forty, and lived just over the back fence.

The Dream

More than an hour later, the insistent ringing of the phone awakened Ben. Sandy was no longer there. She'd covered him with the bedspread from his room and departed on her bike. He kicked it away, weaving unsteadily, still half asleep, to the phone. It seemed to Ben he was now groggy day and night.

The girl with the British-sounding voice was on the line from Seronera saying to please hold for the Chief Park Warden. Ben still didn't know his name.

"Mr. Jepson," the warden said, across half a world. "I don't want to overly alarm you, but we are now very much concerned about your parents. We sent out a search aircraft to the west boundary of the park, out from Kirawira, and found no sign of them."

"Nothing on the radio?"

"I'm afraid not. We're sending out a land search party tomorrow, and I'm hopeful we'll trace them down."

Ben said he couldn't understand why they hadn't made contact.

"Frankly, neither can we," said the warden. "The only thing we can do is keep calling them. On the half-hour from dawn to dark. It's quite possible they've had a radio breakdown and can't answer us. That's happened before in the bush."

Ben asked what else could be done.

"Rest assured we're doing all we can over here. I'll call you the minute we have a report on them. Our search people are quite good."

Hanging up, Ben had a terrible thought: if something has happened, let it be *her*, not him.

Disgusted with himself for even thinking such a thing, Ben went into the bathroom, then to bed, pitching himself in. He remembered he hadn't made the "all's well" walk but decided to skip it this night. For a moment, just before he went off to sleep, he wondered if he was skipping the walk because he was afraid of what was out there, the man with the gun.

Dreams kept winding through his sleep, and he found himself in a neck-high ocean of grass trying to catch up to his fleeing parents. He could see them ahead, the grass bending as they thrashed around in it. He could hear gunshots and knew that the poachers were firing. He could hear himself yelling, "This way, this way . . ." They turned and looked back at him helplessly, then disappeared.

He awakened from the nightmare with a jerking movement, realizing his legs were thrashing, still trying to move through the Serengeti grass. The sheet under him was soaked with sweat, and he lay still, taking deep breaths, waiting for his heart to quit pounding. Some dreams were so real it was a wonder people didn't die in them. He'd remember this one for a while, that look on their faces.

Suddenly, Ben realized he was parched. Fear had done it. He got up, went to the john, then to the kitchen for water. Standing there drinking it, he felt the deep silence of the preserve. Not one of the cats was making a sound. In the distance, he could hear coyotes talking with each other. Closer, frogs serenaded by the lake, as usual.

The clock on the breakfast bar said it was ten to twelve. Between falling asleep on the sofa and going to bed, scarcely two hours had passed, and he was wide awake again.

Fear.

Richie Lewis.

He went to the dining room window and looked out into the compound next to the house. The Bengals were lodged there at present, and he saw Rajah flattened out in the sand, taking advantage of the dampness. Leah was likely at the corner of the house, out of sight, also stretched out.

He wanted to walk up the path and awaken either Luis or Hudson and tell them he had a premonition. Another animal killed. There were no phones in those mobile homes or trailers. But he was afraid to take the walk, afraid there'd be a muffled pop from somewhere outside the perimeter fence, or maybe inside it. Sooner or later, the sniper would shoot at Ben Jepson.

He was a prisoner inside the preserve. They were all prisoners. Richie had laid siege to the acres, and Ben was afraid to move around in the darkness. Maybe Luis and Rafael and Hudson were also afraid but wouldn't admit it.

He went to all the windows, looking out into the shadows, seeing nothing, hearing nothing, and finally went back to bed, staring at the ceiling, listening.

Sleep did not come for a while, and he thought about The Sisters and Rachel, then about his parents struggling in high grass.

THIRD DAY

Rocky

He called Sandy at the Coto de Caza poolside just after he woke up at ten, saying, "You left me. I didn't know you went home."

She was smiling into the phone, he knew, all those freckles dancing around. He could picture her in a sedate one-piece black suit on the lifeguard stand, whistle cord around her neck, puggish nose with a smear of sunblock despite the wide-brimmed hat she always wore.

"You sleep okay?"

The noise of squealing kids was in the background, water splashing.

"I did for a while, then woke up when the phone rang. That warden from the Serengeti. A plane search couldn't find them, and so he's sending a land party out."

"With everything else you've got going on . . ."

"Not their fault," Ben said.

"Their fault for not being here," Sandy said insistently.

"C'mon, Sandy."

"I'm sorry. I'm not being helpful."

Then he heard her yelling on the loud-hailer, "Jimmy, get off that diving board. You know you're too young!"

Almost simultaneously, there was a knock at the front door, and he yelled, "Come on in," then remembered he'd locked it. "Someone's at the door."

Sandy said, "I've got to hang up, too. Call me tonight."

Ben opened the door and Luis stood there, grave look on his face. He said, hesitantly, "Rocky."

He didn't need to say any more.

Ben said, "Is he . . .?"

Luis nodded, and Ben felt the walls close in on him. He heard his own wail, and his fists pounded the breakfast bar. He heard himself yelling, "No, no, no," as if those words would bring Rocky back to life.

Then the sobs began, starting in his chest, wracking it, hurting. He didn't hold them back. Didn't try, didn't care.

Luis eased out of the doorway, closing it gently, and Ben cried for almost twenty minutes, head down on the bar; cried until he was exhausted and no more tears would come.

Finally, he went into the bathroom, avoiding the mirror. His fault that Rocky was dead. He hadn't covered that one foot of open space on the right side of the lion hut, hadn't wired a board in there; gave the sniper exactly what he needed—a clear shot at the lion.

His fault. All his fault.

He went outside, bright sun stinging his eyes, and walked slowly, on hollow legs, to Number Eleven, seeing Hudson, Luis, and Rafael in the compound and, by their feet, the brown-beige body of Rocky.

He went in and dropped down to the cold body, crying

unashamedly in front of the men now, wetting fur. Never before had he felt this way, not even when his grandfather had died.

Hudson finally lifted him up from the corpse, murmuring, "That's enough, Benjamin."

Lifting his ravaged face to the African, he said, "If Richie did this, God help him."

Brave words, he knew, but that's how he felt.

Hudson nodded.

Ben let out a long, shuddering sigh, then said, "Sorry for the tears."

Hudson replied, "I understand tears."

Ben went over to the open space in the fencing and looked up toward the Lewis house for a long time, thinking about taking Richie's life just as Richie had taken Rocky's life.

He heard the CAT WAGN pull up outside Number Eleven and knew that Rocky was going to his grave beside the blue oak.

In early afternoon, well after the burial, Mrs. Mesko unexpectedly drove down into the preserve in her gray Lincoln. She said brusquely, "Tell your mother I'll take her up on that drink she offered me six years ago."

The widow was standing on the porch decking in white slacks and a white blouse, a string of black pearls around her neck, looking like the rich lady she was. Mrs. Mesko was an absolute match for his mother, he thought, someone who could do word battle with Dorothy Courtney-Jepson and might even win. Ruth Mesko was about seventy but still rode a big broad-chested stallion in the Rose Parade every New Year's Day. The Jepsons always watched the parade before seeing the bowl games, and when Mrs. Mesko came prancing along, in all her silver finery, Ben's mother invariably said, "The old witch. I keep hoping she'll fall off."

Ben hesitated a moment, then told the truth. "They're not here. They're in Africa."

"Hmh, you might know they'd be off to Timbuktu," Mrs. Mesko said, looking around. "I've never been down here before. Very pretty." She spoke in words crisp as new lettuce.

"I can get you some iced tea or a soft drink," Ben offered.

"Don't bother," said Mrs. Mesko. "I'll have one when your parents return. I'm really quite sociable when I want to be."

"I'll tell them you visited."

"So now I'll tell you what I came to say, and you can do whatever you want about it." She frowned and stopped. "How old are you?"

"Almost fifteen." He felt fifty-five. He was worn out, even more than yesterday.

"That's old enough to make decisions. I was only seventeen when I got married. Lasted fifty-two years. That was a good decision I made, wasn't it?"

Ben said it was.

"What I came to tell you was that I've thought about your sniper the last two days and remembered seeing Richie Lewis out with a rifle about three months ago. I was riding up near their fence and saw him shooting at paper targets. I recall that his rifle had a telescope on it."

Ben's throat grabbed. Proof!

"I don't know much about guns, although John had a dozen of them, but I know what a telescope looks like. They sit up on top the rifle, don't they?"

"Yes, they do, Mrs. Mesko."

"He was concentrating on hitting those targets so much that I'm not even sure he saw me."

Ben said, "He's won trophies for his shooting."

"Well, my guess is that Richie is the one who's been doing it, damn him."

"We lost another cat last night. Mine."

"Well, Ben, if I was losing cattle the way you are losing lions, I'd go have a talk with Mr. Lewis. If John was still alive, he'd have more than a talk . . ."

Ben nodded, feeling pressure. "Is it all right if I tell Deputy Metcalf what you just said, about him target practicing with a scope?"

"That's why I told you, young man. Tell him to call me if he wants. I'm going to a charity benefit now, but I'll be home by five or so."

Thanking her, Ben watched the tall, white-haired woman get into the shining gray Lincoln Continental.

Proof! At least *some* proof that Richie did have a scope. Added to the fact that Rocky's bullet had come from Richie's side of the fence, there wasn't much doubt any more. No doubt, really.

"Did You Ever Kill Anyone?"

Harry Metcalf was on the phone about four-thirty. "Same rifle, same caliber of bullet, likely the same man." He sounded dejected. His voice was lifeless.

Ben then told the deputy what Mrs. Mesko had said about Richie Lewis.

Metcalf wasn't excited. "Well, we need more than target practice for proof."

"Do we?"

After a prolonged sigh, Metcalf said, "Ben, uh . . . I'm off the case."

"Off the case?"

"The bureau commander made me turn it over to Animal Control. He said we were a people agency. He's right, but not this time. I tried to get him to sign a search warrant affidavit. He refused."

"You can't help us any more?" Ben was stunned.

"Not officially. I've got orders. I have to keep my job, Ben."

"What do we do?"

"First thing, patch that hole in Number Eleven. Isn't that where Rocky was killed?"

"That's already been done. What about Richie Lewis?"

"Just make sure he can't take a shot into any compound. Cut off his fun."

"That's been done, too. We got the bamboo today and have covered all the compound fencing. You can't see into any of them now. The cats can't look out now, either. I feel sorry for them."

"Better sorry than dead," said the deputy. "Keep me posted. I can give you advice. That's about all. Okay?"

"Okay." Ben hung up, feeling more alone than ever.

Even the animals were prisoners now, he thought. But that didn't make sense. They were always prisoners.

Standing there, looking down at the phone, wishing it would ring, wishing he could hear his dad say, Do this! Do that! We'll be home soon!, he felt like running away, giving up.

Invisible walls, not glass, seemed to be closing in on him, and he didn't know which way to turn. Without Metcalf, he now felt completely lost. Suddenly realizing his hands were trembling—something that had never happened before—he bolted outside, standing for a moment in the roadway by the house.

The rolls of wire-laced brown bamboo on the east compound fencing looked forbidding in the harsh, flat afternoon light. As if shielding something bad, the dried cane made the preserve ugly. It didn't seem beautiful anymore. There was a drab, mean look to it now.

The bamboo belt extended around the Bengal tiger compound that butted against the house. He went over, prying a peephole to look in. Rajah and Leah were asleep in the shade, unaware of the evil that was loose in the canyon.

Walking around to the rear of Number Eleven, he moved over to the perimeter fence, forty feet away, and stood there awhile, looking at the rise of cattle land through the chain-links. Over that hummock was the Lewis house. He'd never been up there, had never seen it, just heard about it.

Somewhere over that hummock was Richie, and Ben was again thinking he didn't deserve to live. He'd bullied innocent people all his life. Now he'd killed four beautiful, innocent animals. What's more, he'd turned the preserve into a fort in just three days.

What to do about him?

Go to Frank Coffey and Animal Control?

That was useless. No telling what Coffey would do. Close them down?

Go see Richie and tell him they had proof he was shooting a rifle with a scope on it?

He'd say, "Hey, what's the proof?"

"Mrs. Mesko."

He'd laugh about that, as Sandy had said.

Threaten him in some way, like telling him the sheriff's department was keeping an eye on him.

He'd laugh that off, too.

As he gazed at the sky over the hummock, he thought, *Go beyond what Jilly had said. Wait up by that house in darkness, wait for him to come home from The Cootie, then shoot him. Get rid of him forever. No beating him up, no insane thing like putting him against Dmitri's gate. Just give him what he had coming. Don't shoot to kill. Hit him in the shoulder or legs. Then let him figure out who might have done it and why.*

Ben stood there thinking for almost ten minutes, then walked back into the compound proper, going on to Dr. Odinga's Airstream.

Even in the high heat, Hudson was wearing a shirt. He was under the shade of a silver wattle about fifty feet from his trailer, book in his lap. Ben had seldom seen him without a text of some sort. He studied night and day.

Ben went up to him, asking if they could talk.

Hudson said, "Why, of course," closing his book.

Ben sat down in the sand opposite the canvas chair and its occupant, a man he had considered strange since the moment he'd walked down into the preserve, all of his possessions in a single bag made of what appeared to be Arab carpeting.

"Did you ever kill anyone?"

Hudson was startled. He blinked. "What a question," he said.

"My dad said you killed white men during the Mau-Mau time."

"I don't remember discussing that with your father," Hudson said, frowning widely.

"Did you?" Ben searched his face.

Hudson looked away, obviously trying to decide what to say. Finally, he said, "Many were killed on both sides. We lost many more than they did—thousands."

"But did *you* kill anyone? You!"

Hudson was perplexed. "That was long ago. I was only fifteen, just a boy."

"Boys fought in that war?"

Hudson nodded. "It was truly a war, Ben. We called it a revolution, but it was a war. The British used tanks, machine guns, even bombers. Most of us just had *pangas*, swords. But some had homemade guns. It was a terrible war, but we won. We were fighting for freedom, for independence from the white government, and we finally won."

"And you were fifteen?"

Hudson nodded again. "A boy. I was guarding goats and was recruited by whispers, taken into the Aberdare Forest."

"At fifteen?" Ben had to know the age.

Hudson nodded. "They organized us into raiding parties. They gave each of us a paper to read. It said that every camp must seize and bring into the forest as many livestock as possible. I remember everything the paper said. Destroy all roads, bridges, railways, electric and telegraph wires. Kill as many enemies as possible. Raid the nearest trading center for clothing. Raid the nearest dispensary for medicines. Put on fire as many enemy houses as possible."

"You did all that at fifteen?"

"We all did."

Ben was silent a moment or two, then asked, "Was it a terrible thing to kill?"

Hudson said, dark eyes narrowing, "It was a very easy thing to kill, but it was terrible to think about it later."

"I see."

"Why are you asking me all this? You dig into painful memories."

Rising, Ben said, "I just wanted to know. See you later."

Calling Jilly at McDonald's, Ben said, "I'd like to borrow your dad's .38. Is it loaded?"

135

"Yeah, it's loaded. Why would he keep an empty gun?"

"Will you bring it over tonight?"

"Yeah. What are you planning?"

"Just bring it over. The sheriff's department won't help us anymore."

"Why not?"

"I'll tell you later. Just bring the gun over."

THIRD NIGHT

The Gun

Jilly arrived about eight-thirty, as darkness was again dipping down into the canyon, handing Ben the .38.

"Is the safety on?" he asked.

"Yeah," said Jilly. "You think I'd ride around with a live .38, safety off?"

Ben didn't know anything about guns. Handling it gently, he put it down on the dining room table.

Jilly listened as Ben talked about Rocky and Deputy Metcalf, then said, "Is that why you want the gun? To shoot Richie?"

Ben said, "I want it for protection."

But Jilly knew Ben was lying and said, "We've been friends eight years. I'd never tell on you."

"There won't be anything to tell," Ben said.

"I'll help you," Jilly said. "You know how I hate Richie."

"I know."

Jilly stared at Ben. "You look terrible, you know that? Eyes bloodshot. Face all tight and gray."

"I've felt better. I can see in the mirror."

Jilly leaned closer as if the dining room might have ears. "I'll help you do it. We'll go over there tonight and wait for Richie to come home."

Ben was tempted. He needed someone to stand behind him. But he said, "I'm not ready for that." Involving Jilly wouldn't be right. That gun would be traced right to Jilly's old man.

Jilly went over to the refrigerator and drew out a beer. "Okay if I have this?"

Ben shrugged. Jilly popped it.

Jilly came back and sat down again. "Suppose we do something and get him to come over here. Then shoot him in self-defense. With the reputation he's got, the sheriffs wouldn't care."

Ben laughed weakly. Leave it to Jilly. "Do what to him?"

Jilly sipped his beer for a few minutes. Then he said, "Set fire to his barn, shoot one of his cattle?"

"And he'd know I did it?" Ben said.

"Yeah, he'd know because of what he's doing to you. Tit for tat. He'd get his rifle and come down in here looking for you."

"And?"

"We're hiding in the bushes, and he gets out of the truck with his rifle and *bingo* . . ."

"I shoot him?"

"And I'm the eyewitness. I'll swear I saw him point the rifle at you. The old self-defense case."

"That's like in the movies," Ben said.

Jilly grinned triumphantly. "Like in the movies."

Ben said, "Oh, Jilly," shaking his head. "You should

be one of those mystery writers. You watch too much TV. None of that works in real life."

Jilly said, "You're wrong. I read a statistic that 95 percent of murders are never solved."

"Not with my luck," Ben said. "I just wish you'd come up with a good idea."

Jilly had some more beer, thought a little longer, then said, "Okay, we put masks on, go to the parking lot, get him down, tie him up, and then beat his hands with a rubber mallet. He can't shoot any more."

Ben asked, "Where'd you get that?"

"Out of a paperback last week. *The Body Trade*. A Chinese detective did that to a hitman. Broke all his fingers."

Ben had to laugh.

They heated up a frozen pizza for dinner. Ben had half a can of beer, giving the rest to Jilly. They talked about weight training and football, not about Richie Lewis, then Jilly went home.

When Jilly's headlights disappeared up the road, Ben looked again at the gun. Dark blue, inert on the table, no brain of its own. Just a mechanical device. Only when it was loaded and a finger pulled the trigger was it deadly. He picked it up to feel its weight, then placed it down carefully.

Going into his dad's office, he turned on the lights and scanned the shelves of books, knowing that several were about weapons, bought lately as research for the poaching story. He pulled *Guns of the Twentieth Century*, a large, fat paperback, off the shelf and took it back into the dining room.

Thumbing through it quickly, going past the West

German Beeman/Krico big-game rifles, the Mausers and Sauers, the Steyr-Mannlichers, the Finnish Tikkas, all used in Africa by poachers, he reached the section on revolvers. And, finally, there was Mr. Coombes' .38 "Military & Police" Model 10.

It was composed of a frame, a handle, a four-inch barrel, a trigger, a spring, a hammer. It took eight to twelve pounds of pressure to pull the trigger. The hammer struck the shell casing and the smokeless powder ignited. The resulting gas forced the bullet out of the barrel at around eight hundred and fifty feet per second. It was a very simple mechanism.

Bullets didn't drill perfect little holes. They ripped and tore, smashing bones, often exiting the body in flattened or odd shapes, making gaping holes.

Ben sat for a long while just looking at the blue pistol, thinking about it and what it could do, then got up, took the book back into the office, and replaced it on the shelf. Going back to the dining room, he lifted the .38 off the table, put it into his back pocket, and went out the door for his "all's well" walk, wishing that Richie Lewis would indeed come down into the canyon this very night. The nearly two pounds of metal in his hip pocket felt cold even through the cloth.

It also felt strong. *It made him strong.*

Going along the bamboo-walled east compounds, it occurred to Ben how quiet the animals had been all day. He couldn't remember hearing the usual happy roaring at dusk, the animals talking back and forth between the compounds. They did "talk," his father swore, and that was one of his many investigations. He'd taped hours of the sounds: the whistlelike cries of the cougars, the barks of the leopards, the powerful, plaintive, and sad mating calls of the tigers, as well as their horrendous angry roars. He was working on computer patterns in an attempt to understand them.

Now, there was silence in the preserve, thanks to Richie Lewis.

Ben pried open a peephole in the bamboo of Number Ten, looking at the small pride within. There was more of a moon this night, and he could see them sprawled around on the sand, lifeless. Enclosing them, shutting off their view of the outside world, had subdued them. Shutting off their environment was something his dad had never tried. Maybe he knew already what would happen.

He made the rounds of the east compounds, deciding not to enter any of them. The leopards and jaguars were probably pacing, and he didn't want to see that.

He rounded the trailer area before going down the west compounds and saw that the lights were out in Hudson's Airstream and Alfredo's mobile home. He was certain their doors were securely locked. No lights were on in Luis and Rafael's trailer.

Hurrying now, taking the gun out of his hip pocket, he moved along the west compounds, feeling the wall of bamboo that was near his shoulder rather than seeing it.

He stopped briefly at Number One and again opened a peephole in the canes. Dmitri was pacing, back and forth, back and forth, in the shallow light. Someday he'd gather strength, touch the tiger, and find the invisible sword in his hand.

Hurrying on inside the house, he locked the door firmly and went to the answering machine. There was a message from Sandy. Please call her.

Instead, he went into his bedroom and sat down on the bed in the darkness, placing the gun down on the pillow. He sat there for a few minutes, and then his jaw began to quiver. Without thinking, he wrapped his arms around himself.

He'd never even been in a church. Although he thought his parents believed in God, they weren't religious. When they were home, Sundays were spent in the preserve, his dad out working with the animals, his mother usually in her darkroom. They didn't seem to have a need for religion; maybe they were too busy for it.

All he knew about prayer was that it asked God for help. In the movies, people got down on their knees and closed their eyes. Some said it out loud; others said it silently. He unwrapped his arms from around himself and got down on his knees, put his elbows on the bed, and closed his eyes. "I don't have any religion and I've never been in a church in my life, but, God, I need help just the same. I need help to run this place and the strength to face Richie Lewis. Please look after my parents, both of them. Amen."

FOURTH DAY

Fire

The wind was blowing briskly from the west at dawn, causing the cottonwoods and blue oaks and sycamores to tremble, leaves shimmering in the early light. And not long afterward Luis was pounding on the front door, yelling, "Fire! Fire!"

Running to the door, unlocking it, Ben looked west. The sky was brownish out there, and the smell of burnt brush was already in the air. Once, four or five years back, when the preserve had less than thirty cats, a fire had threatened for several hours. He remembered the near panic of everyone. Fire and wild animals was a formula for disaster.

"How far away is it?" he asked, looking up at the high brown smoke. What other calamity could visit the canyon? Was this God's answer because he didn't deserve help?

"I don't know," said Luis, studying the smoke clouds.

"I'll find out," Ben said. "Get the pumps down to the lake and rig some hoses. Wake up Hudson and the others."

And there was Ben's mother, behind the glass wall, a

143

knowing look on her face. *Let's see how you perform, Ben.*

Luis hurried away.

Ben went to the phone, dialing the county fire department, identifying Los Coyotes Preserve and its location.

The operator patched him through to the operations lieutenant.

"It's about five miles from you, but we expect it to reach there well before noon unless the wind shifts or the aerial water drops stop it. We've got crews out building backfires. It's a mean one. Arson."

Arson. Deliberately set. *Richie,* Ben immediately thought. Had he gone insane?

"What are the chances of a wind shift?"

The lieutenant laughed hollowly. "Few to none."

"I've got animals out here," Ben said.

"I know. Get 'em out of there. You could see fire by ten."

Ben hung up.

Fire less than four hours away. It would take an hour to round up the cattle trucks and another two or three hours to evacuate the cats. Or he could gamble that the wind would change or die down, the water bombers and backfire crews succeed.

His dad had talked about fire and flood from time to time. There had been winter flash floods in the canyon, turning the timid Naranja into a raging torrent, causing evacuation of the animals, but fire was the unthinkable menace. Instructions were tacked on the office bulletin board. They were to pump water from the lake to wet down the grassy area by the perimeter fencing. If the fire jumped the road and got into the cottonwoods, the grease in their leaves and wood would cause them to explode. All the preserve buildings might go, including the house. But much more important, his dad had said, were the lives of the cats. *No gambling.*

While dressing, he glanced out at the bamboo covering on the compound fences, there thanks to Richie. Dry as autumn twigs. If sparks floated down and caught in there, walls of flame would surround the animals. They'd panic; it would be impossible to lead them to safety.

He knew he should have gone after Richie, shot him, not let this happen.

But he couldn't think about that now. He had enough to worry about. The preserve was facing fire by ten o'clock. Bodies would be needed to help load the thirty-foot trailers, people to stand in a double line, with arms outstretched, clasping hands, forming "human chutes." There wouldn't be enough time to erect the portable fencing in front of each compound. Only one cattle truck at a time could enter the space outside the compound gates. Bad design, his father had acknowledged.

First, he called Jilly, asking him to skip work and come help.

"I'll do it if I can shut my eyes," said Jilly. He knew about the "human chutes."

"Not Dmitri," he added.

"Not Dmitri," Ben promised.

Nor would he take the jaguars through the human chutes. That was inviting attack and breakout; and the jags would run free.

Then he called Sandy.

"You think I'm up to it?" she said. "I might break and leave if one charges."

"I'll be there. Luis, Rafael, Hudson, and Jilly will be there."

He heard Sandy taking a deep, uncertain breath. "Okay," she said. Then she laughed thinly. "This proves my love, doesn't it?"

"I don't need proof. See you in a little while."

Next Mrs. Mesko.

"We've got a fire coming," Ben said.

"I know. I've been listening to the police channel. Do you need help?"

"Yes, we do."

Ben figured she'd send a couple of her ranch hands.

Then he began calling the truckers from the list his dad had prepared. Eight cattle cars should be enough; seven carefully placed cats to each car, plus a few in horse trailers from nearby ranches. The problems of mixing known enemies wouldn't allow haphazard cat loading, never jaguars in with the tigers; never leopards in with the cougars; be careful about mixing the males, even some of the females. Otherwise, there'd be fights to the death inside those cattle trucks.

Dmitri would sit out the danger in the cat wagon, by himself, Ben decided; the jaguars could go into a double horse trailer, leopards in another one.

Truckers and horse owners phoned and all arranged while he was chewing on toast, downing orange juice, all rigs promised by eight o'clock or earlier. He left the house and went toward the lake, hearing the throb of the gas-engine pumps. Nearing it, he could see Luis and Rafael manning the high-pressure hoses, fanning water over the grass beyond the perimeter fence. Roofs would be wet down later.

Although gray ash was beginning to float in, breeze

carrying it steadily eastward, they'd have several hours before the likelihood of sparks unless the wind picked up to firestorm proportions. But no gambling, as his father had said. Wet down everything: grass, trees, brush, buildings. Save the animals.

Reaching Luis, whose hands were clasping a nozzle, he shouted, "Trucks'll be here by eight. I'll send 'em to the schoolyard after we load." That was ten miles north, up Los Coyotes. All the vehicles could park there until the danger was over.

Luis nodded.

"It was arson," Ben said. "Richie, I'd bet."

A hundred feet on either side of Luis were Rafael and Dr. Odinga, hosing down.

"Don't worry about Richie," Luis advised. "We have enough to worry about."

Ben nodded. "Let's not even bother with the portable fencing. We don't have enough time. We've got enough bodies. Maybe the truckdrivers will help. We'll try, anyway."

Luis nodded, shifting the thick stream of water to a new area, and Ben ran back to the house to rouse someone from the school district, get an okay for temporary parking.

Sandy arrived, saying, "I'm scared to death."

Ben said, "Don't be. I'll be right beside you. We'll be holding hands."

Hugging, they kissed and continued to hold each other a moment.

Then Jilly arrived, followed by Mrs. Mesko, and Ben put them to work spraying down the bamboo camouflage until such time as the evacuation trucks would roll down into the canyon.

Keyed-up, he felt an odd non-jogging high and was,

admitting it to himself, momentarily glad that his dad *wasn't* there to take charge. Yet he dearly wanted his mother to see him making decisions—right ones, he hoped. He felt good making them. Though a disaster could be looming, it was all strangely impersonal. The fire was capable of terrible destruction, but it was something that could be seen and dealt with, unlike Richie Lewis and his starscope. Richie's presence hung over the preserve like the ugly brown smoke that was drifting across it, high up.

Just before the first truck arrived, he sent Jilly for Luis, meanwhile backing the cat wagon up near Number One, opening the back doors, which would swing inward, allowing Dmitri to jump into the bed of the van if he could be persuaded.

Parting the bamboo, he looked in at the Siberian.

Dimmy was pacing back and forth in long strides, obviously aware something was up. Then Ben realized that the stifling near-silence of the last twenty-four hours, since the bamboo had gone up, was broken. There were now occasional roars and leopard barks, the animals sensitive to approaching danger.

If Dimmy could be coaxed into the van, the only critical part would be moving the van about four feet away from the compound gate so that the back doors of the wagon could be banged shut and locked. The only time the tiger could escape would be during that one second, his huge body crashing against the closing doors. For a fleeting moment Ben now wished that his father were there to handle his favorite cat.

Luis walked up with a skeptical look on his dark face. "I guess we have to do it, huh?" he said, an equally skeptical smile flitting along his shining teeth.

Ben nodded. "Yep. I'm as afraid of him as you are, but we've got to get him out of here."

Luis said, "Rafael is bringing a chunk of meat. We'll put it in the wagon and hope he gets a whiff of it."

Rafael arrived a moment later with a three- or four-pound chunk of cow and shoved it deep into the bed of the van. Then Jilly backed it up tight against the compound gate.

"Okay, let's do it," he said, swinging Dmitri's gate back with a rod, opening the space directly into the cat wagon.

Dmitri stood still, gazing at the open door, then he began to pace.

After a moment, Luis said, "Dart him?"

Ben shook his head. "I don't think so. By the time he goes under, ten minutes, and then we lift seven hundred pounds, you're talking about half an hour wasted on him alone."

Luis tried again. "We go in with him and use Hot-Shots to chase him into the wagon."

Ben said, "No way are we going in there. I got an idea, though. Let's rip off some of this bamboo so he can see out."

"Then what?"

"We get Ricky and have him take a little walk, like a wounded gazelle, up alongside the van, then have Ricky jump into the cab."

The tiger stopped pacing and walked over, still suspicious of the open gate and the barred wagon that was in front of it. He'd taken van trips before and didn't exactly enjoy them. His eyes narrowed with suspicion.

"Get in there, Dimmy," Ben said, loudly.

Jilly was still in the cab, awaiting word to move the

van forward so they could slam the doors shut, locking them securely.

The tiger stared at Ben, then moved slowly away from the open gate, resuming his pacing, gray ash beginning to mar his sleek coat. He looked angry and deadly.

Luis said, "Well, he's sure not interested in that frozen meat."

"We can put it in the oven, but I think it'll take too long to thaw and get bloody," Ben said, racking his brain for a solution.

"Look, Ricky's our best choice. Go get him, and I'll rip some bamboo off."

"Hmh," said Luis. "May work."

There was little danger to the maintenance man, Ben thought. Dmitri had no place to go except into the cat wagon or back into the compound. Ricky would be safely in the cab when it came time to slam the doors, Ben hoped.

He explained it to Jilly.

Jilly said, "You're using him for bait?"

"I have to," Ben said.

In a few minutes, Ricky came limping up to the section of fencing that was now clear of bamboo, and Ben had Luis tell Ricky in Spanish exactly what they were going to do.

"Tell him he doesn't have to do it, but we need that cat in the van," Ben said. "Tell him we need to have him walk back and forth in front of the fence, then walk by the wagon and jump in."

In rapid Spanish, Luis explained to Ricky what it was all about, and the maintenance man grinned and nodded.

"He's happy to help. He feels important," Luis said, but sent Rafael to get a fire extinguisher. The icy white puff could buy a few seconds if things went wrong.

As soon as Rafael returned, Ben said, "Let's do it," looking over at the pacing tiger, mentally crossing his fingers.

Luis said to Ricky, "*Ahora*," *now*, and the gardener began to limp back and forth along the fence.

Dmitri stopped pacing and devoted his attention to the prey.

There was a serious look on Ricky's face. He had a mission to perform. He wasn't exactly sure what his role was, or why, but he had a mission to perform.

"He's moving," Ben said, in a little more than a whisper. "He's taking the bait."

Eyes steadily fixed on the limping man, the tiger came up alongside and fell in step, his huge head turned toward Ricky, the green pupils alight with anticipation of a meal.

"*Siga*," said Luis in a strained voice. *Keep walking.*

"Next time Ricky comes back toward the gate," Ben whispered, "tell him to move slowly along the van, then hop into the cab."

"Okay," said Luis. "Say your prayers."

Ben instructed Jilly. "When I yell *go*, put her into gear and go forward about four feet. Don't stall! Just hit it and stop. Luis and I will slam the doors. Okay?"

There was a muffled "okay" from Jilly as Ricky limped and turned sharply at the gate, going forward alongside the van.

Dimmy, following closely, bounded into the bed of the wagon as Ricky jumped in, and Ben yelled, "Go!"

The van shot forward, Ben slammed the back doors, and Dmitri was safely inside.

Ricky got out, grinning, saying to Luis in Spanish, "You see, he loves me. He followed me."

Luis, letting off a laugh of relief, said "*Sí, sí, te quiere mucho.*" *Yeah, yeah, he loves you, all right.*

Ben grabbed the handyman and hugged him.

Luis grinned. "I never would have thought of that, Ben. Congratulations."

Ben was pleased with himself, at last.

"The trucks should be coming," he said.

The fire was moving relentlessly on a three-mile front toward Los Coyotes in bright red splotches and half-moons along an irregular line, sometimes leaping high when trees were consumed. The smoke was yellow-brown, deep black in some places, and light over the preserve was leaden.

Forest service aerial tankers and several helicopters from the county fire department flew overhead. Ground crews were at work with bulldozers as well as shovels.

Blackened earth and grotesque charred trees and brush, still smoking, were left behind as the wind-whipped flames ate eastward. Trucks carrying crews to build backfires had now descended on the county road.

It was indeed a "mean one," as the operations lieutenant had said.

Ben went inside to call and check on the progress.

"About three miles from you and still moving fast."

The Human Fence

By eight o'clock, the fence was in operation near Number Nine, and the first cattle truck was parked about fifteen feet from the compound gate. Arms outstretched, hands clasped firmly, Mrs. Mesko, Rafael, Jilly, and Luis were on one side; Hudson Odinga, Ricky Castillo, Sandy, and Ben on the other. Luis and Ben were "anchor" men, nearest the truck. The chute formed by the people was eight feet wide.

Ben heard a familiar voice behind him and turned.

Amos Carpenter was standing there, looking sheepish. "Thought you might need an extra hand."

"You bet we do," Ben said, too keyed up to be surprised.

"Don't you dare tell Twist."

"I promise." Now he knew why Amos had winked.

"What are we doing here?"

"Making a fence."

The old man gasped, "Out of bodies?"

"That's it. Just stand beside Mrs. Mesko."

"I thought you'd need me to fight fire."

"Need you more here."

"Take my hand, Amos," ordered Mrs. Mesko.

Ben said, "Stay steady, everyone. Don't move if a cat comes up to you. Luis will keep them going right into the truck. Close your eyes if you want to, but just keep in line. Think of yourselves as a steel fence."

Sandy said, "Ben, my God."

Amos said, "I don't know about this."

Luis had his hog-handler cane in one hand and a Hot-Shot in the other.

Mrs. Mesko said mournfully, "Why did I say yes to this?"

Her ranch hands had everything under control on her acres.

Jilly echoed her, and Ben noticed that Sandy was standing there, eyes tightly shut, lips closed, breathing through her nose.

He didn't blame them, but this was the quickest, easiest way to move the animals. If they stayed in line and didn't break, didn't invite the cat's attention, chances were it would all go smoothly. At the same time, smoke was getting thicker down in the canyon, gray ash falling faster, and the cats were becoming more nervous.

Luis shouted, "Here we go," and swung the Number Nine gate open.

Old Chico came out first, grumbling, tail twitching. He looked at the double line of people and stopped dead.

Ben said, "Come on, Chico, come on," and Luis took the end of his cane and jabbed him in the butt.

The lion grumbled some more, then trotted up the chute and leaped onto the cattle truck loading ramp.

Mrs. Mesko said, "My God, what am I doing here?"

"You're doing just fine," Ben said, laughing a little.

Hudson said, "You can talk about this forever."

"I won't be here forever," snapped Mrs. Mesko.

Mikey then emerged from the compound and did a repeat of Chico, stopping, roaring a few times, scanning the people, until Luis slapped him on the rump and sent him forward.

The final cat of Number Nine, dotty old Henry, did his usual. Instead of plodding straight ahead, he broke through the line under Sandy's arm, and Luis had to circle out, pushing him back toward the truck. He clambered up the ramp and went in.

Once Henry disappeared inside, Ben said, triumphantly, "That wasn't so bad, was it?" He knew that these were among the most mellow of the cats. Others wouldn't be so gentle.

Jilly said, "Are you kiddin'?"

Sandy muttered, "He isn't."

"Well, he sure as hell ought to be," said Mrs. Mesko, ever-crusty. She was clad in old clothes for a change. Ben's mother should see the horse-lady now, he thought.

"I wish dear John could watch me playing kneesy with a lion," she said.

There was taut, nervous laughter from the group as the cattle car was moved on to angle out from Number Ten. The lionesses in there had to be chuted, another time of sweaty palms and closed eyes as the animals came out of their residence, snarling and rumbling, tails flicking.

No one broke, no one ran. And by nine-fifty, when sparks began to fall on the preserve, all the cats were on their way to the school parking lot, including Dmitri, chauffeured by Jilly. Pure luck, for once, Ben knew. Luck more than anything else. Even Jo-Jo and Sergei had behaved.

White hair dotted with black, eyes red-rimmed, face looking as if she'd just come up out of a coal mine, Mrs. Mesko said, "I'm going home. You'll get a bill, young man."

"All right," Ben said, a little bewildered.

Mrs. Mesko broke into laughter. "I'll need two days in the beauty parlor after this." Then she added, "But I wouldn't have missed it." She walked away toward her fine car with long steps.

"And she's seventy," Sandy marveled, shaking her head.

"Maybe more," Ben said.

"More," said Amos Carpenter, his silken white hair also dotted with ashes. "Well, I'm going home, too. Remember, not a word to Twist. She'd skin me."

Ben said, "Never."

Amos grinned. "It was fun. My life's pretty dull." And he walked back toward the Golden Years.

Last to be loaded were the caged aviary birds and the peacocks, Luis getting a chop on the face as he pushed a hooting bird into the cargo space.

As the final truck went up the road, driven by its owner, Ben wrapped his arms around Sandy, murmuring, "We made it."

But as he was saying it, he was thinking, *I made it.*
I did it.
I handled it.
I made the decisions.
We all made it, but most of all, I made it. Me!

And, suddenly, those senseless tears were streaming down his sooty face.

156

Then, sniffing, half-laughing, wiping water with the back of his hand, he took his Zacatecas straw off and said, "Lookit this. My hat's shot. It's ruined." The broad straw was gray-black with ash.

He dropped it to the ground and stomped on it. He'd never felt better in his entire life.

He felt unmediocre for a change.

He hadn't cracked, hadn't broken.

He'd kept it in the road.

A little before eleven, the fire marched up to the edge of Los Coyotes Road, directly across from the preserve, sending up showers of sparks. Two of the cottonwoods caught, bursting into flames. Luis and Ben watched the county crew directing water into the trees, and then they all moved around the preserve with shovels, watching for embers.

By noon, the danger was over.

Ben said, "If I'd known the fire was going to stop at the road, I wouldn't have shifted the cats."

Hudson Odinga said, "How could you know?"

The smell of fire was still thick in the air, and across the road there were charred monuments to it, stumps and tree trunks; the earth had a crust of black. But it had not disturbed the preserve. Nothing had been lost.

"Each of those cattle trucks will cost us eight hundred dollars," Ben said.

"When the boss comes home, he'll see how close it came and will say you did the right thing," Luis said.

"I hope."

"You'll see," said Luis.

Ben walked up to the hardtop to thank the fire captain

and the crew. They were mopping up on the opposite side of the road.

"We're lucky," said the captain. "The wind went from gusting up to forty down to ten in the last hour. Otherwise, this fire would have swept right on through you and gone for another thirty miles until it hit desert cactus."

"I hear you think it was arson."

"We don't think so. We know so. There was a witness. A big guy in a white pickup truck set it at first light. Tossed some gasoline around, matched it, and drove off."

Richie! It had to be Richie. Ben's heart drummed harder. Big guy! White pickup!

"Did they get the license number?"

"I don't know. The arson investigators are on it."

Ben nodded, wondering whether or not to tell the fire captain about Richie. Better to tell Metcalf, he thought. Metcalf knew the history.

"Okay to move our cats back?" he asked.

"Anytime you want. Fire's over."

"We'll do it after we get something to eat," Ben said.

Standing nearby was the last person he wanted to see this day. Frank Coffey. There he was in his green knit shirt and khaki pants and black boots, black notebook in his small, soft hands.

As Ben walked by, he said, "You people get a permit to move those cats?"

Ben said, "No, we didn't," and kept walking.

Murder

A few minutes after the jaguars, the last of the cats to be returned, were inserted into Number Twelve, Ben checked the answering machine and then flopped down on the couch. No call from Seronera; none from Metcalf. He didn't bother to shower; he'd wake up in an hour or so to do that and eat something. He went to sleep almost immediately, every muscle aching, head feeling heavy.

The phone was insistent around 7:00 P.M., and Ben got up groggily to answer, elbows leaning on the breakfast bar, eyes closed.

"You called me, Ben?"

Deputy Metcalf.

"Yeah. Yeah, I did."

"I hear you dodged some fire this morning."

"Yeah, the wind died down. We got lucky. I still evacuated all the cats. Cost us a lot of money."

His knees felt wobbly, and he moved a few feet to sit on one of the high stools, trying to clear his head.

Metcalf repeated, "You called me?"

"Yeah, the fire captain told me it was arson and that there was a witness who said a big guy with a white pickup did it. *Richie*, Deputy. That's who." Finally.

There was a moment of silence on the other end, and then Metcalf said, "Ben, Richie didn't do it. Richie is dead."

Ben's feet slid to the floor. "Dead?"

"He was killed last night about eleven o'clock. Drove into a tree about three miles north of the Arco station."

"Are you sure?"

"I saw his body."

"He's dead?" The Jepsons' mortal enemy was dead! Everyone's enemy was dead?

"Ben, he was murdered. Someone forced him off the road and into that tree."

Ben was wide awake now. "Murdered?"

"Murdered! He didn't set any fires at daylight, believe me."

Ben was speechless; didn't know what to think, what to say.

"We studied the tire marks, and another vehicle bull-dogged him right into that tree."

Ben was stunned.

Metcalf said, "Ben, anyone out there do any driving last night?"

Ben's mind wasn't functioning.

"You hear me?" Metcalf said.

"No, we didn't," he said.

"Can you prove that?"

"I think so," Ben said.

"Check around," Metcalf said. "You sound like you're half awake."

"I am."

"Talk to you later," the deputy said and hung up.

Richie dead, after all the years of harassment. Ben found it hard to believe. He stood by the stool a long while trying to collect his thoughts. Richie murdered?

Luis was the only person at Los Coyotes with a driver's license, but he had no car. Of course, he could have borrowed one. Some of Mrs. Mesko's hands had old cars. Now and then, he borrowed one, Ben knew.

Richie dead! Unbelievable.

In the twilight, Ben walked slowly up to Luis and Rafael's trailer. The two men were eating outside as they usually did in the summer. They had a table near the corner of the trailer.

Approaching them, Ben said, "Richie was killed last night. Someone ran him off the road near the Arco."

Luis's dark eyes registered no surprise. He swallowed his food and said, slowly and deliberately, "Whoever did it deserves a medal. He needed to die."

Luis quickly told Rafael what had happened.

Rafael grinned and said, "*Bueno, bueno!*" *Good.*

"Were you out driving last night?" Ben asked Luis.

"Not me, *señor*," said Luis, the dark eyes boring and direct. "I was very tired. I went to bed."

Ben said, "Well, we can't blame Richie for setting the fire."

Luis said, expressionless, "No, we can't do that, can we."

On his way home, Ben checked the cat wagon to see if there was any fender damage or streaks of white paint.

None.

The only other car at the preserve was his parents' black BMW. The keys were on a hook in the kitchen. It

161

was parked in the exact spot where his father had left it two weeks before.

Ben called Larry Templeton to tell him what had happened to Richie Lewis.

Larry was shocked, too.

FIFTH DAY

Expert Witness

On the phone, just after eight in the morning, Larry said, "I was thinking last night about who else might have it in for you if it wasn't Richie."

"Me?" Ben asked, startled. "Have it in for me? Personally?"

"No, not you," Larry said. "Your father, the preserve, the cats."

"Well, the only other guy we've thought about is George Trilby, who has the property next door. He runs that little grocery up the road. He's hated us since we moved in."

Larry said, "Well, maybe it's someone nobody has thought of."

"Like who?"

"Someone you don't even know. Your dad has never talked too much about anything threatening except maybe viruses. But I remember he did tell me quite a while ago about a civil suit in Norfolk, Virginia, when he was filling in at the National Zoo."

163

Ben was only a baby when they'd lived in Washington, and neither of them had ever talked very much about those two years when his dad was at the National and his mother was beginning to build her own career as a photographer. Ancient history now, misted over.

Larry went on. "He was an expert witness for the defense, an insurance company, as I recall. A lioness had mauled a little girl, and the plaintiff, a sailor stationed in Norfolk, lost the case. After the trial was over, the sailor shot and killed the defense attorney. Seems to me he also threatened your father in some way. He was judged temporarily insane. I spent hours last night trying to remember what insurance company it was, the name of the attorney. Thirteen, fourteen years ago, I believe. He ever tell you about that?"

"Nope," Ben said, mystified.

"Well, the sailor went to prison but may be released by now. Look in your father's files and see what you find."

Another turn, another twist. Ben learned more about his parents from magazine articles than he did from them. They seldom talked about themselves except to reporters or on TV.

"Let me know if you find anything," said Larry.

"Okay."

"And speaking of your parents, what have you heard from them?"

"Nothing at all."

"They're all right, I'm sure," said the vet, after an uncomfortable pause.

"I hope," said Ben, not feeling very hopeful at this point.

"Keep me posted."

Ben knew what an expert witness was—Dr. Peter Jepson was sometimes asked to testify in legal actions involving animals—but his dad had never mentioned a Norfolk trial or a sailor, and Ben had never explored those file cabinets in the office. He'd never had a reason to go into them.

Temporarily insane? Out of prison? Maybe it had been a mistake to strip the bamboo screening off the compounds yesterday, put the cats back into their front-row homes?

Putting the answering machine on "record," Ben went out into the sunlight. The tree leaves danced. With the light breeze coming from the west, there was still a strong burnt smell down in the preserve. Likely it wouldn't go away until the first good rain in the fall. But now the cats had visual freedom again, could look into each other's residences, see what was going on; could look out through the fences at birds or at Ricky with his wheelbarrow. They'd immediately seemed happier, he thought, as he walked the pathway beside them.

He paused at Number Fourteen.

Six young cats were in there, and one in particular, Nimbus, had always drawn his attention. Nimbus looked a little like Rocky, though he'd never be as handsome. But his large eyes revealed intelligence, and whenever Ben entered Number Fourteen, Nimbus was always first to come to him, rubbing up against him, showing affection. He came bounding to the fence this morning, and Ben pressed the back of his hand up to the chain-link to receive the rasping kiss. "How ya doin', Nimbus?" he said, and then went on.

Luis was getting ready to go on the routine fence

check, make sure there were no overnight holes in the chain-link, when Ben walked up.

"Larry Templeton thinks that maybe someone we don't even know is doing the shooting. Some ex-sailor who killed a lawyer and threatened my dad a long time ago. Some court case. They said the guy was insane."

"*¿Próximo qué?*" said Luis, shaking his head in wonder. *What next?*

Ben sighed and muttered, "Who knows, Luis. What's next? I'm so tired of all this."

"Insane guy," Luis said, frowning.

"Maybe? I've got to look in the files, see if there's anything about him. I'll do it later." He turned away, then turned back. "Nellie has her chemo at ten."

Luis nodded as Ben headed toward the house.

He still wanted to run and hide this morning. Just run, go as far away as possible. Cash a big check out of the business account, go to Hawaii or Tahiti. Just run. Far away.

The hell with his parents, the hell with the animals. Whatever happened at Los Coyotes, let it happen. He'd had it.

He went back past the compounds without even looking at the cats, much less speaking to them, not wanting to see them, feeling anger. They were the cause of it all.

Oh, no, they weren't! No, they weren't! Peter and Dorothy Courtney-Jepson, the jet-setters, were the cause.

They'd collected the big cats.

Locked them up!

Made them the targets!

Then they'd left him to deal with this mess.

Inside the house, he thought about placing a call to the Serengeti, just to check again, wanting to yell at his

parents, but it was already nearing ten o'clock at night over
there.

The tiny red light on the phone recorder was blinking
accusingly, persistently, and he listened to Frank Coffey's
miserable voice asking for Dr. Jepson to please call back.

He shouted, "Up yours, you jerk," and rewound.

Nothing that the Animal Control man had to say was
urgent. Likely, he wanted to know if the cats had been
shifted back.

Yes. Yes. Yes.

Then he called Sandy out by the Coto de Caza
poolside.

"You want to go to Tahiti?" he asked, angry edge in
his voice.

"When?" The usual kid yelps and splashing noises
were in the background.

"This afternoon, tonight."

"How about tomorrow?" she said, with a laugh.
"What's happened?"

"One thing after another. Larry thinks an ex-convict
might be the sniper."

"What?"

"You heard me."

Sandy's laugh was low and hollow. "Any word from
dear Poppy and Mommy?"

"No!" He practically yelled it. Then, after a beat, he
said, "I'm serious, Sandy. I may just get the hell out of
here."

"Don't do it until I come over tonight."

"It depends."

"I love you," said Sandy.

"I love you, too," he said, wearily.

Then Ben went on to Number Eight and led poor Nellie over to the cat wagon. She moved along lifelessly, head down. The other cats watched. Ill, she was prey. Law of the Serengeti. He had the feeling that she wouldn't be around when his parents returned. When and if.

With Luis driving toward the animal oncology center in Mission Viejo, twenty-odd miles from Los Coyotes Canyon, neither of them paying much attention to Alfredo's cassette of Willie Nelson singing "Rainy Day Blues," Ben thought of what Larry Templeton had said about the court trial, the sailor. Maybe there *was* something in the files about it. He'd start on them in the afternoon, take his mind off Seronera, off the dead animals.

And he was, in fact, always learning something new about Peter and Dorothy Courtney-Jepson, those part-time strangers who had conceived him on a love cot in the *kopjes*. Things they'd never bothered to tell him! But he supposed it was that way with a lot of kids. He'd never asked. Live a quarter of a lifetime with your folks and know them very little. Of course, there were other parents who wouldn't shut up about the old times. Which was worse? Not knowing was worse, he decided.

Luis finally turned the cat wagon into the center, which was equipped for radiation, chemotherapy, and cancer surgery, a depressing but necessary place to go. Larry Templeton had given Ben's dad a choice—put the lioness to sleep or try to send her into remission for a while.

"If we can get her into remission with chemotherapy, she'll feel much better and have a good quality of life for many months," Larry had said.

Dr. Jepson chose to try remission, naturally.

Ben said to Nellie at the back of the wagon, "Come on, baby, let's go see the doctor."

He wasn't certain about the good quality now. But she did jump over to the concrete platform, and then he led her inside the center, with its hospital smells, hearing the muffled barks of penned dogs from the clinic next door.

The oncology specialist, a vet named Jacobs, examined Nellie and then said, "You know it's a losing battle, don't you?"

Ben nodded, looking down at Nellie.

She was on her belly, staring off vacantly. He stroked her head.

Dr. Jacobs said, "Why don't I call your father? I'd strongly recommend euthanasia at this point. I think her immune system is almost gone."

"He's overseas," Ben said.

"Oh?" said Dr. Jacobs. "When will he be back?"

"I'm not sure," Ben said. "Soon, I hope."

"Well, it isn't something that has to be done today or tomorrow. But I'd say you should make a decision, for her sake, within a week. I don't think she's getting much pleasure out of these final days."

Yet another decision. Ben said, "I'll talk to Dr. Templeton."

Jacobs nodded and went over to prepare the chemo shot.

Ben scratched along Nellie's head, and she responded by turning tired brown eyes toward him. She wanted to die. That was obvious.

She took the shot, and then he led her out, hoping not to come back to this place again.

Nellie flattened out in the rear of the wagon, and Luis drove silently on back to the preserve. Ben missed eagle-eyed Rachel at his side. He fought off tears, knowing he should have told Dr. Jacobs, "Yes, it's time for Nellie to sleep."

FIFTH NIGHT
Sniper

There were eleven old steel-gray file cabinets in the office, a converted bedroom at the south corner of the house. In late afternoon he began to pull manila folders, stuffed with papers, out of the first file. It was marked 1967–1968 in a slot below the handle. Twenty years old, the papers gave off a musty odor and had already yellowed.

Part of the early Serengeti period, he saw, before the Washington National Zoo. The correspondence was mostly about foundation grants and the need for money. Some scientific papers. Way over his head. Not much personal stuff. But he already knew he wanted to go back over all these papers, slowly and carefully. A history lesson about the two strangers he lived with.

The drawers in the next cabinet, 1969–1970, contained files about their first book, text by Dr. Peter Jepson, photographs by Dorothy Courtney. Ben suddenly realized he'd never read that first joint book, published years ago, only looked at the pictures. His dad seemed so young, as did his mother, in the jacket photos, posed with a lion. She was so pretty. He put the 1967–1968 file folders back into their cabinet, thinking, finally, that this was the way to find out about his parents.

Sandy arrived about six-thirty, when the cats were serenading, their roars bouncing off the boulders. She had brought two deli submarines, some macaroni salad, and potato chips. Ben brought icy 7-Ups out of the refrigerator to join the subs on the breakfast bar while Sandy shoved Angela Winbush into the boom box and "You Had a Good Girl" came out.

Ben wasn't all that wild about Sandy's tapes, and she wasn't exactly wild about Willie Nelson, Dan Seals, the Gatlin Brothers, or Kenny Rogers. However.

They began to eat, four years of files nearby on the floor. Nodding toward the folders, Ben said, "Larry thinks there might be something in there about this sailor who threatened my dad around fifteen years ago."

"What kind of threats?"

"Don't know."

"He wasn't in Vietnam, was he?" Sandy asked, trying to figure the years.

"Who?"

"Your father?"

"No, it was just during that period, Larry thinks. I've gone through two years. I can't believe those files, Sandy. They were actually poor then. Really poor. I'm telling the truth. My mother borrowed money from her family. My dad was writing to all those foundations asking for money."

"Dorothy and Peter Jepson wanting? Hah!"

"They needed money to stay in Africa."

Sandy's eyebrows went up. She swallowed a bite of sandwich and said, "Africa, you might know. Not someplace plain like Atlanta or Boise, Idaho."

Ben said, "Okay, they've come a long way." Trying to change the subject, he said, "I'll take '70 and you take '71. We're looking for a lawyer from Norfolk, Virginia."

"Plain old Norfolk."

Ben ignored the dig. He didn't agree with her this time. She could knock them for the recent years but not for the early ones. He remembered the early years, when he was close to his mother, as good ones. "They've come a long way," he repeated.

They finished eating and then took the "all's well" walk, saying little to each other. They spoke to the animals and didn't see Luis or Dr. Odinga.

Back at the house, Sandy changed to Depeche Mode. "Fly on the Windscreen."

Ben thought the lyrics didn't make sense.

Sandy went over to the file folders, head nodding to the beat.

"Next one to the end," he said, clearing up the paper plates on the formica bar, wiping it clean so they could spread papers on it.

They sat side by side on the stools, reaching into the folders, scanning papers, placing them face-down, sometimes talking about what they were reading.

"Here's a letter from William Holden, addressed Dear Peter and Dorothy . . ."

"Holden had a place in Kenya."

A little later, she said, "Wow! Book-of-the-Month Club bought *Lions! Lions! Lions!* They got rich. Hey, this is fun to read."

Fun? Ben wondered about that. He'd never thought about the files being fun.

It was nearing nine when Sandy said, "This may be it. Several letters to Peter Jepson from a Norfolk attorney named Lee Shepperd . . ."

Ben put aside a newspaper clipping from the *Washington Star* about his dad being appointed as interim director of the National Zoo, dated August 20, 1973, the year after Ben was born.

The November 1973 letter Sandy was holding began, "Thank you for your report on the safety precautions of the Halsey Zoo . . ." Then there was another letter, referring to a phone call, saying that "the Thomas Hedgepeths had filed a damage suit against the Halsey Zoo for fifteen million" and that Shepperd hoped that he (Dr. Jepson) would be willing to serve as an expert witness. Trial date expected the next year.

The file was almost four inches thick and contained not only letters and newspaper clippings but full transcripts of the trial testimony, the appeal, and the sentencing of the accused.

A Shot

The story of Thomas Hedgepeth was laid out on the bar, including *Virginian-Pilot* newspaper accounts. There were photos of little Chrissy, of her mother Thelma, and of the big bosun's mate, Thomas, the war hero. Staring at Thomas, who looked rugged and forbidding, Ben wondered if he was the sniper. He hadn't seen that face around the area, though age would have changed it, of course.

There was a photo of lawyer Lee Shepperd. None of his dad. The last story told of the guilty plea, due to temporary insanity, for the murder of Shepperd by the ex-Navy man, and his sentencing to prison for life with the possibility of parole. The legal community thought the sentence would have been lighter if the victim hadn't been a prominent attorney.

There were the thick transcripts of the entire trial.

Heads almost touching, both bent over the bar, they read all the clippings, Sandy turning slightly to look at Ben with a frown when a *Pilot* article about Dr. Jepson mentioned an illegitimate son.

Ben had thought only the three of them shared that secret.

Take it in stride, he told himself.

Swallow it.

Pretend he didn't notice.

Almost at the same instant, he decided—face it; this was Sandy.

"That's me, the little bastard," he said to the side of her head, almost a throwaway line, as if he didn't care.

She turned, disarmed, eyes soft, voice soft. "Who else? You're an only child, aren't you?"

"Yep."

"Doesn't matter to me," she murmured. "I'm only glad they had you."

He said into her hair, "I'll tell you the whole story sometime."

"You don't have to."

They embraced for a moment, and then, taking a deep breath, Sandy said, "Back to work!"

"Yeah, okay." Ben sighed.

"You think he's out of prison now?" she asked.

"We'll try to find out in the morning. I'll talk to Metcalf, show him all this." All except the interview.

"With this one, it's scarier than ever, isn't it?"

"I guess." But somehow, strangely, he wasn't feeling the breathtaking fear he'd felt with Richie Lewis. Maybe that would come later. For now, there was a face and a possible name for the sniper. Maybe that face and name would go with the bullets that had sliced into the preserve.

"Metcalf said that one of those nightscopes had been stolen from the SEAL's base down in Coronado five or six months ago. The FBI told him. This guy's an ex-SEAL. Connects, doesn't it?"

Sandy gave Ben a "beats me" look, then said, "Maybe that insanity wasn't so temporary."

"Maybe."

She went on, "You know, reading these clippings, I have some real sympathy for him. He lost his little girl; his wife divorced him. Everything went wrong when he came back from Vietnam."

"I know."

"You have to think he was really out of his mind when he killed that lawyer. Driven to it."

"Yeah," Ben said, again looking out the picture window toward the compounds, which were now unprotected on both sides, cats still such easy targets. "But if he's come out here for revenge, that's something else. If he's the guy who killed Rocky, Rachel, and The Sisters, I have no sympathy at all for him. If he's the guy who set that fire, I've got no sympathy for him. Two ranches burned; a horse had to be destroyed. Probably take that land five years to get back to normal. If he's that guy, I want him in jail."

"Ben, only a day ago you thought it was Richie."

"So did everybody else. Now, I think maybe it's this guy, and if it is, I hope what happened to Rocky will happen to him. Right in the heart."

Calling Larry Templeton, he said, "I think we've found him—a sailor named Thomas Hedgepeth . . ."

"That's the man," Larry said, excitedly. "I remember that name. Keep me posted."

Ben said he would.

Reaching over for his father's thick black book of phone numbers, he found the Santiago Canyon Sheriff's Substation and dialed the number, asking for Deputy Metcalf.

"Not on duty tonight," said the bored voice on the other end.

"Can you please give me his home phone number. It's important."

"Can't do that. Against department policy. Call him Monday 'less you want to talk to someone on duty. What's it about?"

Remembering that Metcalf had been taken off the case, Ben hung up, thinking they should put the bamboo fencing back up immediately. Just for safety. They didn't need any more cat deaths. He'd call the deputy Monday.

Sandy had been looking in the South Orange County phone book. "No Hedgepeth listed here. That's an unusual name."

Without answering, he dialed 411. When the operator came on, asking "What city, please?" he said, "Don't know," spelling the name out. "Just South Orange County."

After a moment, she said, "No one by that name listed in South Orange."

He drove Sandy home in the cat wagon about ten and took the newspaper clippings to bed with him. Slowly and carefully he again read the article about his father. Dr. Jepson was aloof and stony-hearted in the story, an uncaring zoologist who testified for insurance dollars. Ben knew better. Then he came to the part about himself.

According to New York gossip columnist Earl Wilson, Peter Jepson and Dorothy Courtney, the lovely photographer, have a two-year-old secret named Benjamin. They aren't married, of course. Shame on them, Wilson said.

The column was dated 1973.

Until now, it had never bothered Ben that they hadn't gotten married until well after he was born. Had this story forced them to do that, get married? It was like a cold gust of wind from under a long-shut door. Or perhaps it had always bothered him and he wouldn't recognize it?

Turning out the light, he was awake for quite a while before he fell asleep. About eleven some of the lions roared to break the canyon stillness and then the sounds tapered off as usual, diminishing, fading back to silence.

The strident sound of the kitchen alarm cut into his brain, and Ben jumped out of bed. Either the main gate system or the conduit on top of the perimeter fencing. Whichever it was, someone was tampering or trying to get inside the preserve.

He grabbed his pants off the chair, wriggled into them, grabbed the .38 off the nightstand. Pausing only long enough to pick up the flashlight, shining it briefly on the pistol to make sure the safety was off, he ran out the door. The reaction to the fence alarm was basics, finally. His subconscious had primed him to act as he stayed on the near edge of sleep.

A quarter of the way to the gate, a chuck of wood flew off an oak beside him, hitting him in the shoulder, causing him to cry out in pain and surprise. As he dove to the sand and rolled, he could hear the whine of the ricocheting bullet. Ending up behind the tree on his belly as another chunk came off, another whine splitting the quiet, he knew he'd made a mistake coming out alone.

Whoever was up there, Thomas Hedgepeth or not, had total command with that starscope.

Ben hugged against the bark, with no idea of even

trying to use the .38 to duel with the rifle. He was panting heavily even though he hadn't run very far. Heart slamming again. The Richie Lewis fear had returned. He looked at the yellow hands on his watch—4:45. Almost the same time as the first attack on Los Coyotes.

He didn't move until he heard a car starter grinding away up on the road. Then, jumping up, dodging through more trees, he raced up the short hill as the engine finally caught.

He was in time to glimpse a white vehicle through the perimeter fence. Running without lights, going north, it appeared to be a pickup. That's what Richie drove, but Richie wasn't around anymore.

Watching until it vanished, Ben turned and slowly went back to the house as the first rose light broke in the east. He sat in the living room like a zombie, .38 in his lap, until it was daylight. There was no sympathy left for the ex-sailor. He was hanging around Los Coyotes to kill.

The big cats soon began their early morning chorus, starting in the compounds at the far end.

It was Sunday.

SIXTH DAY
The Islamabad Sword

Sunday was usually a lazy, sleep-in day for all, big cats included. Chopping meat for the late afternoon meal could be delayed for several hours. Only the daily fence check had to be done, but even that could be postponed until noon. Yet Ben did not hesitate to awaken Luis and Hudson Odinga about seven. Briefly, he told them what had happened by the blue oaks and what he'd learned from looking over the files—the Thomas Hedgepeth business.

"Shot at you?" Luis said, frowning widely.

"You should not have gone out there," said Hudson, also frowning. "You should have awakened me, Benjamin."

"I wanted to catch him," said Ben.

"And get yourself killed," said Luis.

It was over, so there was no use talking about it, Ben thought. "Let's get the bamboo back up on the fences," he said to Luis.

The Chicano groaned. "Today?"

"I say again we should go up on the road and lay in wait for him," said Hudson. "Ambush him."

That was getting to be a better and better idea, Ben thought. "I'm going to try Deputy Metcalf at home."

"I thought he was taken off this," Luis said.

"He was," Ben said, emphasis on the *was*.

At a few minutes after nine, Ben drove the cat wagon up along the edge of the dirt road in front of 145 Villa Vera Cruz, in Trabuco Villa, a place of scattered middle-class homes, mostly old. Many of the people who lived in Trabuco Villa had horses. It was an area of citrus and avocado trees; tall eucalyptus.

Since it was another back-roads trip, Ben took the chance of driving without a permit.

Hedgepeth file in hand, he walked up to the door of the faded barn-red cottage, almost hidden by cascades of pink bougainvillaea. A woman in her late forties or early fifties answered the knock—Mrs. Metcalf, he guessed—saying, "He's out in the shop. Go up the driveway."

Ben could hear machinery when he approached the garage, then saw Harry in a sawdust-spattered gray smock, bending over a wood lathe and what looked to be a table leg shaping up. Metcalf's face and eyebrows were dusted with fine wood particles. So this was what cops did on their days off? Made furniture.

He called out, and the deputy glanced around, turning off the lathe. Frowning, he asked, "How'd you know where I lived?"

"The girl at the desk told me. She knew who I was."

"More cats shot?"

Ben said, "No, but I got shot at this morning, Deputy, and I think we know who's doing it."

Metcalf laughed abruptly. "Sure isn't Richie Lewis."

"I have some stuff for you to read."

Staring over his safety glasses, Metcalf said, "Now, Ben, you know damn well I got kicked off this case."

"But you said it was because it dealt with animals."

"That's exactly right."

"Well, I'm human, and he was shooting at me. I can show you chunks out of an oak."

Metcalf took off his safety glasses.

"Okay, let's see what you have."

The littered shop, rich with the smell of wood, had power tools—band saw, drill press, joiner, the lathe; all sorts of hand tools hanging from hooks. Sawdust was everywhere, even up in the spiderwebs. Against one wall was a dusty, spring-poked black leather couch, and Metcalf said, "Take a seat," reaching for the correspondence and clippings.

Almost thirty minutes passed before Metcalf looked up and said, "I see what you mean."

Ben said, "I tried to get a phone number for him last night, but he wasn't listed."

"If he busted parole and came out here, you can bet he changed his name, changed his looks. You can buy a new ID over in Santa Ana for a hundred-fifty. Driver's license, the works. He's spent twelve years in prison; he's not about to go walking around as Thomas Hedgepeth."

"I thought maybe he'd be easy to find."

"We've got people who've busted parole, broken out, or are on one or another wanted list for fifty years, and we still haven't found them. Just luck when we do. It's not that hard to take up a new life anymore. Used to be that everyone knew everyone else. Now, we're just a lot of strangers."

183

Ben said anxiously, "But that doesn't mean you won't try to find him?"

"First, I've got to find out whether he's pardoned or on parole or just broke out. I'll call Richmond; then I'll see if Sacramento has a Thomas Hedgepeth driver's license or registration. I'll do what I can, I promise."

Ben's hopes tumbled, even though he knew law wheels were usually on slow speed. He'd thought that Metcalf, after reading everything, would have an all-points bulletin issued on Thomas Hedgepeth by afternoon.

"Now tell me more about getting shot at this morning," said Metcalf.

That wasn't difficult to do.

"You're sure it was a white pickup?"

"It was white, and I think it was a pickup. It was pretty dark out there, but I think it was a pickup."

Metcalf ended by asking, "What do you hear from your folks?"

That wasn't difficult to answer, either.

"Come on inside while I call Richmond," Metcalf said. "I may not be able to reach the guy I want."

Inside the deputy's house were a lot of white pine antiques and lace curtains. The kitchen smelled as though they'd had sausage and pancakes for breakfast. It seemed like weeks had passed since Ben had eaten a good breakfast.

Metcalf had a speaker phone system, so Ben could hear both sides of the conversation. Identifying himself as a sheriff's deputy in Orange County, California, the deputy asked for the name of the parole officer who'd handled Thomas Hedgepeth. He got it, and the home number back in Virginia, then dialed, introducing himself to Foley Stevens and saying, "Sorry to bother you on a Sunday."

Stevens said, "We're in the same business."

Metcalf said, "I'm calling about a Thomas Hedge-peth . . ."

"Yeah, I was his examiner. I recommended parole and the board granted it, but now he's on our wanted list for violation." He had a Southern accent, honeyed and slow.

"How long ago did you let him out?"

"Can't recall the exact date, Deputy," Stevens said. "I'd have to look at the records. But I'd guess six or seven months ago. He was supposed to report to his parole officer in Norfolk but never showed up."

"I think he's here now," Metcalf said.

"Oh? You got him in custody?"

"I wish we did. I think he's playing revenge games out here with a man who testified as an expert witness in a civil suit a long time ago."

"The one where his little girl got mauled?"

"That's it."

Stevens laughed wryly. "We all thought he'd gotten that out of his craw. That's what got him in here, shooting the defense lawyer on the case."

"I know. I just read all the clippings. What kind of prisoner was he?"

"Model, after the first year or so. But he was one that no one messed with. Kept himself up physically. Hard as a rock. I saw him once in the prison gym. He's in his forties and has the body of a twenty-year-old, big tattoos on his biceps. Kept to himself most of the time, I was told. But you can never really figure what's inside someone's head, can you?"

Metcalf said that was right. "Did a shrink get to him before you granted parole?"

"You bet," said Foley Stevens. "I can call you tomorrow and read off the psychiatric report, but as I remember, there was something about residual guilt over the death of his daughter. He'd never fully recovered from it. But how could you expect him to? Anyway, the shrink also recommended parole."

"Is all that stuff in the newspapers about his Vietnam combat record true?"

"So far as I know. It was submitted by his lawyer at the trial."

"You think he's dangerous?"

There was a long pause in Richmond. "Hard to say. I think he's capable of being very dangerous."

"That's what I wanted to hear," said Metcalf.

"What's he done out there, if it is Thomas Hedgepeth?"

"Sniped four animals in a private zoo run by that expert witness, then shot at the son this morning. I know he's using a starscope, which fits in with his SEAL background. The real target, I think, is a zoologist named Jepson. He's overseas at the moment. The kid is running the place. He heard the alarm early this morning and went outside. The guy was just trying to scare him, I think. The kid was duck soup with that nightscope. The guy took some wood out of a tree instead of shooting him."

"You want me to send you a copy of my file?" Stevens asked.

"Yeah, I'd sure appreciate that, Express Mail," said Metcalf. "How's the weather out there in Richmond?"

"Raining like the devil. How is it in southern California?"

"Sunny and hot."

"You might know," said Stevens.

After Ben got home, he called both Sandy and Jilly.

Sandy said, "Oh, my God, you could have been killed."

Not much question about that.

Leave it to Jilly to say, excitedly, "He hit the tree? Oh, I gotta come over there."

"Later," Ben said. He had things to do.

Try Seronera. Talk to Hudson. Help with the bamboo fencing. He found the Latinos strapping it on over the chain-link by the Lewis property.

He got around to Hudson in late morning. The Kenyan was in the washer-dryer room up by the animal hospital.

"The fewer the better," he advised. "Just you and myself, Benjamin."

"Not Luis, Rafael?"

Hudson shook his head, transferring washed clothes to the dryer, setting the timer. "The fewer the better," he repeated. "Don't even tell them."

Studying his face as the dryer began thumping away, Ben said, "I have a gun."

"The dart gun?"

"No, a real one. A .38. It belongs to Jilly's father." He didn't say he'd had it out last night, by the oaks.

"Bring it," said Hudson. "We'll go up there after dark and just wait. All night if necessary."

He was going behind Metcalf's back to do this but thought Hudson knew best. More experienced than Metcalf, he knew how to ambush, how to fight at night.

Walking away from the laundry with quick steps, Ben felt excitement, anticipation, a tingling in his stomach, a faster pulse beat. At last they were going to *do* something—not just be easy targets for some madman; not just talk or think about him. All right, Metcalf wouldn't approve, but maybe they could get lucky and deliver the sailor to the deputy.

The path to the house led by Dmitri's compound, and Ben stopped by the fence to say hello, putting the back of his hand against it. The Siberian got up lazily from his resting place to pad over, muscles flowing like yellow-black paint. He was making the "ff-fouf" purring sound. So gentle a sound, so unlike this huge, dangerous animal. The prickly tongue was warm and wet through the chain-link.

Would the courage and determination of these daylight hours follow on into the night? Ben knew he'd be thinking about it all afternoon. Would he back out at sundown, let Hudson go up there alone? He hoped not.

Avoiding Dmitri's eyes, he looked down the supple length of the tiger, thirteen feet from mottled pink nose to tip of tail. If only the great cat could will Ben his strength and ferocity.

Tyger! Tyger! burning bright . . .

Suddenly, he had the strangest feeling about Dimmy. The longer he stood by the fence thinking about the night ahead, the more urgent it became to enter Number One and finally touch him. If his dad could do it, so could he. If Sandy wanted to call it "rites of manhood," let her. If he could go into the compound, touch the tiger, and come out unharmed, then going up to the road with Hudson would seem less dangerous. Perhaps Dmitri had been the key to his fears all along. By touching him, he'd be armed with the symbolic Islamabad sword.

Did any of that make sense? Probably not. But he felt compelled to go in there. *Now, today.* Whatever the risk.

Sorting out the keys on the brass ring, he found Number One and moved the few steps to the gate, feeling the greenish eyes track his every step.

He inserted the key into the padlock and said to the tiger, "Dimmy, I'm finally coming in. Be kind to me."

The locking arm fell free, and he lifted the gate latch, slowly opening it, looking toward the far end of the compound, aware that the tiger was still by the fence, still watching.

Remembering from long ago, when he met his first tiger, his father had said, "All right, slowly close the gate behind you and just stand there, Ben. Don't look at him. Look anywhere but at him."

Ben was now about two feet from the gate, his back to it, hands down by his sides, sensing that Dimmy was motionless, too—oriental slanted eyes, different from lion eyes—staring at this boy who'd dared to enter his space.

Time stopped.

In what seemed like forever, Ben could hear bird chatter, cars along the road and the far-off whine of jets, the distant babble of voices. He looked up into the hot, cloudless sky, sweat trickling down his forehead. Though it seemed an hour, ten minutes went by before the tiger moved.

He came slowly across the sand, passing in front of Ben, ignoring him, going twenty or thirty feet further, then stopping.

Ben couldn't resist a quick glance and saw that Dimmy had his head turned away, was looking into Number Two at the lionesses. Then the big head began to turn, and Ben cast his eyes back skyward, knowing the tiger was coming his way again.

In a moment, the seven-hundred-thirty-pound animal

was only inches away, and then Ben felt his right foot being pinned down. A paw was on it. He could smell the tiger, feel his high body heat.

The heavy paw stayed in place, and Ben slowly moved his right hand, touching the Siberian on his back, saying quietly, "Okay, we're friends."

After his foot was released, Ben reached behind and opened the gate, slowly backing out of it, taking with him the invincible magic sword from Islamabad.

The wavering voice of the Chief Park Warden at Seronera, said, "I finally have a report for you, Mr. Jepson. Can you hear me?"

"Yes," Ben said, the world ceasing to spin around for a moment, his grip on the phone tightening.

"A search party found your parents' campsite but not them."

"Where are they?"

"We don't know, to be very honest."

"You don't *know?*"

"Apparently, they were attacked by poachers. Their radio is destroyed, and the vehicle is gone. They may be on foot. The poachers may have taken the Land Rover. But there's no sign of bloodshed in the camp itself, which is good. Looting, yes."

"When did it happen?"

"Seven or eight days ago, we estimate. Now we know why they didn't communicate. The radio is smashed beyond repair."

"And no one has seen them since?"

"I'm afraid not. But we have another search party out looking for them. My own hunch is that the poachers took them twenty or thirty miles away from the camp and then dumped them, warning them to go home."

Ben imagined his parents being forced out of the Land Rover, fierce men in battered safari hats pointing guns at them, then driving off. Or a worse scenario: shooting them dead and driving off.

"Are you using helicopters?" Ben asked. If they were on foot, slow choppers instead of aircraft would seem best.

"We're in the beginning of the dry season over here. There's smoke and haze over the grasslands. Not much visibility. Ground search has the better chance. Motorized."

"And you have no idea where they are?" Ben's lips began to stick together, mouth flour-dry.

"Well, we think they're north and west along the border, traveling in that direction, heading toward the Mara, trying to keep clear of the poachers."

"The Mara?"

"A river."

"My father knows quite a lot about the park." Ben didn't know what else to say.

"I'm aware of that," said the chief warden. "All to the good. Once the searchers contact us, I'll call you immediately."

Same as before. *Wait it out, Ben. Be cheerful. Be optimistic.*

But on hanging up, he had an awful feeling that the next call from Seronera would say that his parents had been located: dead.

"I'm so very sorry, Mr. Jepson," the Chief Park Warden would then say.

Ben didn't feel like "Mr." Jepson. Didn't feel like a kid. Didn't feel like an adult. Didn't know what he felt like.

Run!

Ben was on his back in the coarse high grass on the slope down to the perimeter fence, alongside Hudson Odinga, thinking how really dumb this was—in darkness, lying in wait with a Kenyan for convicted killer Thomas Hedgepeth, batting off night bugs and mosquitoes. Had he talked himself into this or had Hudson done it? Both, he thought.

The fire had burned all cover from the opposite side of the road, where they should have been in hiding. Until the flames marched to the macadam, there'd been high weeds over there, as well as wild lilac, pampas grass, and cane, eight or ten feet tall, huge blooms silken and yellow-white. Plenty of places to hide and wait. Now just blackened earth and gray ashes lay alongside that shoulder.

The high slope grass up from preserve property was the second best cover, Hudson had said when they came out through the main gate as blackness gathered in the canyon.

This seventh night was going by slowly and painfully, ending an unreal week. It seemed impossible that only six days had passed since the peacocks screamed early Tuesday morning.

Could his mother see him now, at eleven o'clock, flashlight down by his hip, Hudson silent beside him, bony black hand cuddling the .38, she'd probably say, "Ben, are you crazy? Letting Hudson talk you into this? Hedgepeth'll blow the two of you to kingdom come."

That's what Ben thought she'd say, and he was tempted to get up and go back to the safety of the house. This *was* insane, he knew, as insane as the sailor might be.

"Let Harry Metcalf stop him, for God's sake. That's what he's paid to do," she'd say from behind her glass wall.

His father, knowing Rocky, Rachel, and The Sisters had been shot, would say, "Go get him, Hudson and Ben."

No, none of that was right. They were both running for their lives along a border in the Serengeti. They had their own problems.

"I went in with Dmitri this afternoon," he said to Hudson.

He'd called Sandy right away to tell her, and she said, "You didn't!" and "You're crazy!" and "Are you all right?" not mentioning the "rites of manhood."

He'd told Luis. Openmouthed, Luis had said, "*Me estás dando atole con el dedo.*" *You're kidding me along.*

He'd tell Jilly tomorrow. Jilly had been busy the whole day making Big Macs and French fries.

Most of all he wanted to tell his father. Soon.

Hudson lifted his head. "Why?"

"I had to," he said. "I'd been thinking about it a long time. I had to touch Dmitri. The Islamabad legend says if you touch a tiger, a sword will spring into your hand and you'll be invincible."

Hudson grunted. "You're lucky to be alive tonight." He didn't buy the legend.

Ben said, "I don't think he's as fierce as everyone says."

Hudson didn't answer. He'd never been too talkative and hadn't said very much, except about Dmitri, since they'd come up on the road at eight-thirty when the last shallow dusk began to die over the low mountains to the west.

Sparse daytime traffic had thinned even more. Maybe a car every twenty minutes, half an hour. There'd be a whine of tires, a brief splash of light down the embankment, and then the engine sound retreating. After midnight, there'd likely be only one an hour.

Looking at the stars, Ben said, "Suppose he stops his truck right up above us."

"I hope he does," said Hudson. "If he has a rifle, I don't want him fifty or sixty feet away. I want him five or six feet away, your flashlight shining in his eyes, blinding him."

"Then what do we do?"

Hudson said, matter-of-factly, as if it would be easy, "Take the rifle from him and march him down into the preserve. Then you call that deputy sheriff friend of yours."

Too simple, Ben thought, even though he had no experience in an ambush. "Hudson, he's a combat man. You should read what I read about him. He got a lot of medals for what he did in Vietnam."

"I got none in the Aberdare, but I'll match his experience in guerrilla tactics night for night."

Now that they were up by the road, burrowed down in the grass, what had sounded so good in daylight suddenly seemed foolish, no matter that Hudson was a freedom fighter. The sound of wood chunking out of the oak was still strong in Ben's mind. Hedgepeth obviously knew how to handle rifles.

Up close or at a distance.

Ben awakened with Hudson's lips at his ears, whispering, "He's here. Right above us. He just stopped. Get up when I say and be ready to shine that light right in his face."

In the damp grass, Ben was stiff and cold. For a few seconds, he was also disoriented. Then a jolt of memory told him they were about to ambush the sniper.

Hudson whispered, "He's still in the truck, probably waiting for his eyes to adjust."

A moment later, they heard a door squeak open and then gently close.

"Up now," Hudson said.

Ben glanced over and saw that Hudson was in a crouch, holding the .38 with both hands.

Then Ben got up and also went into a crouch, hearing the slam of his heart, grasping the flashlight, right index finger on the button.

Hudson whispered, "He's coming round to this side."

The next sound was the right-hand door opening, and Hudson said, "Now!" then yelled, "Stay where you are!" to the sniper.

Ben hit the switch, and the powerful beam locked on a bearded man standing by the half-open door, looking down the slope, eyes wide with surprise, one hand inside the truck, reaching for the rifle stock. In the instant of surprise, he reminded Ben of a big cat suddenly caught in a tube of brilliant light, blinded momentarily, freezing there. Of Rocky last week.

Ben got a good look at the eyes and nose and blond-gray beard, metal-rimmed glasses reflecting, left hand on the cab roof.

Then, in a display of agility that was hard for the eye to follow, the big man dove into the truck through the half-open door and in a split second they were the hunted, not the hunters. The rifle barrel appeared, resting on the window frame.

Ben dropped the light as Hudson yelled, "Run," and they took off for the preserve gate, scrambling along the edge of the perimeter fence, two figures frantically trying to escape through the night. A bullet twanged and made yellow-red sparks along the upper part of the chain-link. Only the incline of the slope saved them.

They ran through the gate and down to the safety of the oaks, standing with their backs against the rough bark of a tree, panting. Another bullet pierced the oak, a parting shot.

In a few minutes they heard the truck start off and go north.

There was nothing to say, each stunned by the turn of events, each feeling foolish, and they parted in front of the house, Ben going inside and Hudson continuing on to his Airstream, hiking his long body up the pathway, fleeing defeat.

There was no magic sword.

SEVENTH DAY

Rent-a-Cop?

In the morning, Metcalf was in the bureau commander's office at the Santiago Canyon Substation saying to Claire Means, "I want back on that preserve case."

Ben was sitting outside and could hear them.

"Look, Harry," said Means.

The deputy interrupted, "The guy with the nightscope is shooting at humans now. Night before last and last night. I've got a make on him, I think. Murder in the second degree paroled out of Richmond, Virginia, about six or seven months ago. He may be a psycho."

Captain Means grunted unhappily and said, "You sure you know what you're talking about, Harry? I'm sick of that animal story."

"Tell you what, Claire, if somebody gets killed out there—that boy, for instance—it's going to be in your lap."

"Is that a threat?"

"No, sir. Cold, hard fact."

"Okay, Harry, you're back on it. But if I find out it's

another repeat of some lion or tiger getting shot at, I swear to God you'll be on traffic detail until you retire."

"Fair enough," Ben heard Harry Metcalf say before walking out of the bureau commander's office.

Outside, he said to Ben, "C'mon with me."

They went back to Metcalf's office, and he called the prison psychiatrist who'd examined Thomas Hedgepeth. The deputy sat at his desk in the cubbyhole and talked into his phone box, taking notes.

Said Dr. Steinman, "If you're asking me if revenge is psychotic, I can only tell you that it can be but not always. There are millions of people who exercise revenge but aren't psychotic. Most everyone has practiced revenge at one time or another, petty divorce to spilling blood. Thankfully, the latter isn't common."

The deputy said he understood.

"If you're asking me specifically if Thomas Hedgepeth is a psycho, my answer is a qualified no. Of course, I haven't seen him in six months, but I doubt he's changed very much."

"Did he talk at all about the trial or the little girl?"

"Not about the trial, but I did ask him if he still felt guilt over his daughter's death. He admitted that he did, which didn't surprise me. He'll never get over it."

"Did you talk to him about killing the attorney?"

"Briefly," said Dr. Steinman. "He regrets it. Genuinely, I think."

"Because of the time he had to serve in prison?"

"That's involved."

"Does it surprise you that we think he's out here to do a revenge number on the expert witness at the trial?"

There was a low laugh in Richmond. "Nothing really surprises me anymore. I've been practicing too long."

Metcalf said, "The reason I think he's some kind of nut is that he started off out here shooting lions."

"That doesn't necessarily make him a nut. That belongs in the eye-for-an-eye, tooth-for-a-tooth category. Goes back a long time before it went into the Bible, Deputy."

"But will he progress into shooting humans?"

"He's shot one already. That attorney. I do suggest you get him back into custody as soon as possible, just in case . . ."

"Could he have brooded all those years in prison?"

"Absolutely. But unless he volunteers to talk about it, there's no way that I have to guarantee he'll open up. He can say, 'I have no bad feelings,' and I can't dispute him. I don't do these parole interviews under lie detectors. I wouldn't if I could."

Ben sat there listening, beginning to feel as if he knew Thomas Hedgepeth.

"You're aware of his Vietnam background?"

"Of course, I'm aware of it. He was trained to kill. That simple."

Looking over at Ben, asking more to himself than to the psychiatrist, Metcalf asked, "But will he kill again?"

Dr. Steinman replied, "I can only repeat, get him back into custody as soon as possible . . ."

Ben stood beside the artist in the sheriff's department headquarters building in Santa Ana, saying, "Make it a little thicker on the sides."

He was talking about the beard on the face of Thomas

Hedgepeth. The artist had blown up the *Virginian-Pilot* photo of the sailor and was now using what looked to be large crayons to add hair to the cheeks and chin.

"You're sure about the color?" asked Deputy Metcalf, standing on the other side.

"I'm sure," Ben said. "Blond and gray. Like my father's beard, only his is shorter."

"What else could you see?" asked the artist, a woman named Watanabe.

"His glasses. They had metal frames."

"What color metal?"

She took up a pencil.

"Silver colored."

"Shiny?"

"No, not shiny."

Glasses appeared on the nose of Thomas Hedgepeth.

"What else?" said Metcalf.

"A blue cap."

"What kind of cap?" the artist asked.

"Like policemen wear."

"A cop's cap?" Metcalf's voice contained disbelief.

"I think," Ben said.

"With an insignia on it?"

"Yes."

Blue and black crayons now began to quickly fill in the cap and visor. It took several minutes.

"Okay, what else?" asked the artist.

"I was aiming the flashlight beam at his face, into his eyes, and it all happened so quickly, but I think he was wearing a uniform of some kind. Also blue."

"Blue uniform," Metcalf repeated. "A jacket?"

"Yeah, a jacket."

200

"What kind of jacket?"

Ben frowned. "Like a cop's jacket."

"I'll get that in a minute," said the artist. "Let me finish the cap."

They watched silently as she juggled the blue and black crayons, combining the colors. Then she began to fill in the body. After about five minutes, she said, "How is that?"

"Looks like what I saw last night."

Metcalf said, "Ben, you think that could have been a security guard's uniform, not a regular cop? One of those rent-a-cop guys you see guarding private communities, sometimes stores?"

Ben nodded. "Like that, I guess."

Miss Watanabe said, "I'll take my time and redo this to scale if you'll tell me how tall he was."

"Okay, now the size of this guy," Metcalf said to Ben. "Was he as tall as I am?"

"Much taller. I'd say five or six inches taller than you are."

"I'm five-ten," said Metcalf. "That would make him six-three, six-four."

Ben nodded. "Yeah."

"Big shoulders?"

"Yep."

"How about his eyes? You see the color?"

"He was wearing those glasses. I just know they seemed to be boring at us."

Metcalf said to the artist, "He has blond hair, so make 'em blue."

In about fifteen minutes, the retouched photo, and the drawn-in body to scale was completed, and the deputy said, "Okay, Ben, take a final look. We'll go to press with this.

Meet Thomas Hedgepeth. I don't know what name he's using at the moment, but this is your man, okay?"

Ben said, "That's him, all right."

On the way back to the substation, riding the Santa Ana Freeway in the deputy's gray sedan, Metcalf said, "Tell me again what you remember about the vehicle."

"It was white and old. Looked a lot like what Richie Lewis used to drive."

"Chevy, Ford, Dodge?"

"Can't tell you. I only saw the tail end of it as he went up the road."

"Going north?"

"Yeah."

"When you saw the same truck last night, or what looked to be the same truck, which way was it headed?"

"North."

"So we can make a guess that he lives somewhere north."

Ben said, "Yeah, I guess."

"Anything else that you can tell me?"

Ben was silent a moment, then said, "Not that I know of."

Metcalf looked over. "Okay, I'll tell *you* something. Going out of the house Saturday morning, when you heard that alarm, was dumb. Letting that African talk you into trying to catch Hedgepeth last night was even dumber. Both of you could have been killed."

"I know that now," Ben said, contritely. "I wasn't using my head. I just wanted to get it all over with before my father came home. My fault, not Hudson's. He was just trying to help."

"Anything else happens out there, you call me. Don't

go askin' those Latinos or that Dr. Odinga for law enforcement advice."

"I won't."

The gray sedan took the El Toro off-ramp and headed east, past the little shopping plazas and fast-food places that lined the road on either side. McDonald's, where Jilly worked, was along there with Fuddruckers and Pollo Loco.

"And return that .38 to your friend. Easy to get hurt or hurt someone else with a gun, especially if you don't know how to handle it."

Ben felt as though he was being treated like a ten-year-old. "I'll give it back."

Metcalf glanced over again. "Don't sound so low. We'll catch this guy, sooner or later."

Ben wasn't all that confident.

"Peaks and valleys, that's what life is all about," said Metcalf.

"I'm tired of the valleys," Ben said.

"Know how you feel," Metcalf replied.

EIGHTH DAY
McDonald's

Ben met Sandy in the hot, still late morning at McDonald's, just off El Toro Road, on Bridger, across from the nursery that bought the dried lion dung. Luis and Ben had hauled in nine bags, and Ben had a check for ninety dollars in his shirt pocket. Luis had crossed the cat wagon underneath the freeway to take Graciela over to see Alfredo for a few minutes.

Ben said they'd have lunch and wait for Luis to return.

Jilly was behind the counter in his forest-green uniform, with his Big Mac visor on, acting super-efficient and bossy, bucking for assistant manager.

"I'm surprised those girls don't kick him right in the tail," Sandy said. "Look at him, cock o' the walk."

"He's just acting like that because we're here and he knows we're watching him."

They were sitting directly opposite the order counter with its three steady lines of customers. Chicken Mc-Nuggets, with sweet-and-sour dip, were being pushed this week on Bridger, along with desserts, including the new Chocolaty Chip Cookies.

They were watching the lines. Barefoot guys in shorts and girls in short-shorts. Hair in curlers. Tank tops. Muumuus. Old geezers in black socks half up white hairless calves. Fat men, fat women. Fat girls, skinny girls. Knee-high kids. Lots of T-shirts.

With this backdrop of hungry humanity occupying stage-center, a big, bearded man in khaki shorts, a blue tank top and go-aheads, tattoo on his right bicep, moved left to right to dump his tray into the garbage container.

Ben couldn't believe what he was seeing. "It's him," he blurted, feeling his chest tighten.

"It's who?"

"Thomas Hedgepeth! I'd know him anywhere," Ben said, looking at the beard, metal-rimmed glasses, broad shoulders, and powerful legs. The ex-sailor was striding toward the door.

Ben said to Sandy, "Go outside; see which way he goes."

She was half up, too, bewildered. "You're going to follow him?"

"Go outside."

Then he moved quickly to the counter, bypassing the line, hearing protests, saying to Jilly, "Give me the keys to your car."

"For what?" Jilly frowned.

"Just give me the keys. Quick."

"For how long?"

Some guy behind yelled, "Whatta you doin', man?"

"I don't know how long. Just give me the keys."

Still frowning widely, Jilly tossed him the keys, saying, "What's this all about?" as Ben raced toward the door.

Outside, Sandy said, "That's him."

She pointed to a white Chevy pickup waiting for the

light two hundred feet away, turn signal indicating he'd go left on El Toro Road.

"You sure?"

"I saw him get into it."

Ben frantically searched the parking lot for Jilly's fire-engine red VW. "You see Jilly's bug?"

"Is that it in the back row?" Surfboard rack on the roof, it glittered in the sunlight.

"Yeah, that's it," Ben said, running.

Sandy was only a pace behind. "Why Jilly's car?"

"Luis may not be back for half an hour."

"Ben, why don't you just call Metcalf?"

"I will, once that guy stops somewhere."

They reached the bug. It was locked. Another two seconds to unlock and turn the starter. Sandy climbed in, saying, "This is crazy."

The bug screeched backwards, and they shot out on to Bridger, made the green light, turning left on El Toro, accelerating to forty. Traffic was heavy, as usual.

"If he keeps going straight, we'll catch up," Ben said, feeling a booming in his chest.

"Ben, suppose he looks back and sees you. He knows who you are. He's seen you with that telescope."

"I'm not getting that close."

They were passing cars to keep up, scooting in and out of lanes.

"Hope a cop doesn't get behind us," she said, looking back.

Ben looked over. Her hands were tight balls in her lap.

"Me, too," he said, braking for a light at Bunbury, then springing ahead of the pack when the green light flashed. He caught another red at Willard and then went to fifty, really risking a ticket, after the Trabuco intersection. He was sitting forward on the seat, muscles strumming, tight as drawn bowstrings.

Sandy spotted Hedgepeth first, on the curve where El Toro bent toward Pebble Creek. "There he is," she said, breathlessly. "On past that black car."

"I see him," Ben said. "Okay, we'll just keep him in sight. That's all."

"What if he stops?"

"We'll stop. You'll find a phone and get to Metcalf while I keep an eye on him."

"How do you know he doesn't have a gun with him?"

"I told you we're not getting that close."

Ben could feel the tension building in her, matching his own. He glanced over again for a side view. Her freckles were tiny brown dots on a field of white. Her lips were pursed, jaw extended. One hand now gripped the dashboard above the glove compartment. It didn't help to see her that way. Sandy was usually the collected one.

Finally, she said, "Why don't we get closer, get his license number, then drop back and phone Metcalf?"

"And lose him? It might take them a week to find him."

They moved swiftly eastward, passing by gold-colored cattle land along Rancho Canada de la Alisos and Alisos Creek, what there was of it. Dry, all summer long.

"He's got a decision to make up ahead," Ben said. "Turn on Live Oak or keep going on Santiago. I'm betting he'll stay on Santiago and then take Los Coyotes. Either way, I'm going to pull up on him."

"Not too close, Ben," Sandy warned. "He'll get suspicious."

"A guy and a girl in a bug? C'mon, Sandy."

"Okay, Superman. It was you he was shooting at, not me." Her voice cracked with nervousness.

Ben closed to within six car lengths. Hedgepeth's license plate was 2J62854. "Write it down in case we lose him."

Sandy opened the glove compartment to find a piece of paper and sucked in her breath as if she'd touched a snake. "You know what's in here?"

"What?" Ben glanced down and over but couldn't see what she was talking about.

"The gun. The one Jilly gave you."

"He was supposed to put that back under his old man's bed."

"Is it loaded?"

"Yes, it's loaded. Never mind. Just get the number written down."

Reaching around the .38, she fished out a napkin.

"I almost feel I know him after reading all that stuff," said Sandy, looking ahead.

"I was thinking the same thing a while back." Those two pages in the *Virginian-Pilot* had taken Hedgepeth from the time he was a child right up to the night he shot the attorney.

Suddenly, the pickup slowed down, and Ben almost ran up on him, braking hard, searing rubber.

Then Hedgepeth floored the gas pedal, taking off like a jet.

"He's spotted us, Ben," said Sandy. "Let's turn around."

Ben had the bug floored, but the VW didn't have enough horsepower to keep up with the pickup, and the sniper drew steadily away.

Up ahead, past a sharp curve, was Camarillo Road, a dirt loop, access to an electric power station. But Ben didn't think Hedgepeth knew enough about the area to take it; hide back up in there.

"I don't think he spotted us," Ben said, knowing that he did.

"Well, why did he slow down, then jump ahead?"

Ben didn't answer. He rounded the curve and dropped to fifteen miles per hour at the intersection to the power company road.

"Don't go in there, Ben. He could be waiting."

Ben heard the shrill near panic in her voice and said, "Okay. But we lost him."

Ahead was a tanker truck and beyond the truck several passenger cars. No white pickup.

"He just took off and left us in the dust," Ben groaned. "I should have kept up with him."

"Thank God you didn't. He saw us, Ben! I swear he saw us! He was looking in his mirror when he slowed. He knew he was being followed."

She was right, but Ben wouldn't admit it. "We'll find him," he said, stubbornly.

All of a sudden Ben made an abrupt U-turn and drove back to the loop road.

Sandy asked, "Where are you going?"

"Up in here," he said, moving onto the dirt.

"He's probably waiting for us, Ben."

He dropped the speed to ten.

"I can punch it and whip around on a dime," Ben said, mind made up to catch him.

Ben noticed she sat there silently fuming.

They got to the top of the loop and the fenced-in power

station. An employee was cutting the grass area, and Ben stopped, jumped out, and ran over to the fence.

"A guy come up here in a white pickup?" he asked.

"Yeah, stayed about five minutes, then took off."

"Guy with a beard?"

"Yeah."

Ben ran back to the VW and ducked in again.

"Ben, for God's sakes," Sandy cried. "*I don't want you to find him.* Let's get to a phone and call the deputy, give him the license number."

"I want to know where he's living. That's all. Has to be somewhere near here." Find him, then call Metcalf.

Sandy shook her head. "If I'd known you were going to do this, I wouldn't have gotten into the car."

Jilly's shining VW whirred along at sixty, back on Santiago, sun flashing off the polished metal.

Less than a mile ahead, Los Coyotes Road intersected with Santiago. Four miles on north was the preserve. Sixteen more miles and Los Coyotes jogged back into Santiago. Past the preserve was the Golden Years, then Trilby's store; after that, three small villages interrupted the desolation, squatting forlornly along the macadam and, finally, another trailer park, the Silverado, site of a big drug bust last year.

"You want me to drop you off?" Ben asked, glancing over at her, meaning at her house.

She returned his look, staring with frustration, and took a long time to answer. "No, but I want you to promise me that we won't go near him, no matter what. You'll call Metcalf? No fancy stuff with that gun. Okay, Ben?"

"Okay."

"And if we don't find him?"

"I drive you home."

"Great. My day off blown," said Sandy.

They kept driving into the back country, past Sandy's house, past Mrs. Mesko's, heat waves rising from the asphalt.

Ben glanced to the right as they zipped by the preserve. The main gate was closed, hopefully locked. The cats couldn't be seen from the road. All was well down there, he thought.

On by Golden Years and Trilby's.

Silverado Trailer Park

About a thousand people lived in the mobile home communities of Winterwood, Somerset, and Soquel, with five hundred in Somerset, the largest. The homes were mostly two or three bedrooms. Unlike the Golden Years, they permitted children. They were family communities.

Ben's mother called the first two "yokel towns." Saturday mornings dogs and kids were piled into the backs of pickups to go into El Toro and shop at K-Mart. Soquel was almost entirely Latino.

Ben drove into Winterwood, which had five or six gravel streets, going slowly, searching for the white pickup.

Sandy said, "This is stupid. They're all over the place."

"Look for that license number."

"And have him walk out and see us?"

Each time they spotted a white truck Ben had a tiny cardiac arrest until they passed it.

"Dammit," said Sandy—just a general angry, frightened dammit because of what they were doing.

Ben was beginning to wish she wasn't along.

They cruised slowly through the streets of Winter-wood, all named after women. The guy who developed it must have had six or eight daughters. They came out of Wendy, not having seen a white pickup with license plate 2J62854.

Where in the devil was Hedgepeth hiding?

Ben drove back out on Los Coyotes Road and traveled the three-quarters of a mile to Somerset, which had a mini-mall fronting it. Gas station, 7-11, hardware store, branch post office. There were twenty or thirty streets in that village, all paved. Somerset was the upper crust of the yokel towns. Campers and boats were out in front of some of the homes, dirt bikes and three-wheelers, plastic kiddie pools—all roasting in the sun, under the cloudless sky.

Sandy finally said, "You know, he could be looking out the window of one of these houses."

"Or he could be sitting on the front step with his rifle," Ben said, defiantly. He *had* to find him.

"It's ninety degrees," Sandy said, as if that had some-thing to do with the hunt.

But for the first time Ben noticed the heat.

He'd never been up inside Somerset. The town was laid out in a rectangle, east to west, and he went to the far side, the south, then drove up and down each street. They must have seen a dozen white pickups, of all vintages and varieties. None was the vehicle belonging to Thomas Hedgepeth.

"Two more places, and I'll take you home," Ben said.

They went on up to Soquel.

"I doubt he speaks Spanish," said Sandy.

213

"He doesn't have to speak Spanish to rent a place here."

Silence again as they traveled the two miles and turned off into the Latino community. His mother called that one "taco town." There were only twenty or twenty-five homes on ten graveled streets, and Sandy was right. There were no pickups parked in Soquel. The men were off working.

Ben stopped at the edge of Los Coyotes Road. "I think I know what happened."

Sandy turned toward him, mouth drawn in a tight line. "I've had enough of this, Ben," she announced.

Ignoring her, he said, "When we went on past that dirt loop, he went up inside, stayed four or five minutes, came back out, waited for us to come by, then took off up Santiago."

"I don't care how he did it," Sandy said.

"He kept going on Santiago, then turned back at the Los Coyotes jog. He's in that Silverado trailer park, that's where."

"You know that for fact?"

"I don't know anything for fact. But we're going to check out Silverado."

She looked away and shifted in the seat, wild with anger.

His mother had no name for Silverado Oaks, which was actually set in a grove of tall eucalyptus. The oaks were long gone. There was eukie smell in the air. The tall Australian trees gave off a scent of incense in hot weather.

The trailer park consisted of forty-odd spaces, and most were occupied by permanent welfare families. It was almost a shantytown. Unpainted plywood add-ons were coated with dust. Ben had been in there once with his dad. A trailer had been for sale, but they didn't buy it. It was in awful condition.

Broken-down cars were on every lane. The swimming pool looked as though it had cracked in an earthquake ten years ago and had never been fixed. Rubber tires dangled from ropes in the children's playground, the swings long broken. Here and there were a few geraniums, red petals dimmed with dust.

Ben parked alongside the road, several hundred yards from the entrance.

He said, "Leave the motor running."

"What do you mean?" Sandy asked.

"I'm going to walk down in there."

He remembered from before that there was a narrow entrance, about three cars' width, into the park. He wasn't sure about the lanes in there but thought he could dodge through the trailers on foot and get back out to the road in case he was discovered. Taking the VW down, he could get tangled up, blocked in.

Ben said, "Get over here in my seat and keep this thing in gear in case I do have to run for it. I'll jump in, and we'll take off."

"You're sure?"

"Yeah, I'm sure."

Ben got out and walked up toward the entranceway to Silverado Oaks.

He could see down into the park from the road shoulder. Nothing much had changed since the last time he was there. Maybe it was grubbier than before. In contrast to Somerset Village, it seemed lifeless.

There was an arch over the entranceway. Some of the pink plaster had chunked off. Heavy chains, once white, now rusted, went down either side of the three lanes. A hut, over to the left side, had an Office sign above it, but the door was off; window busted. Nobody in it.

Feeling as though he was walking on land mines, Ben went under the arch and began looking for the old white pickup. Six or seven trailers straight up, he saw a man bending over the engine of a car. The hood was propped open.

To the right, by the empty swimming pool, two little children played on the rubber-tire swings. They were going back and forth, not talking or laughing.

Hedgepeth's truck wasn't down the center lane of the park, so Ben went to the right and began walking along that row, seeing cars but few people. They were inside, he guessed, trying to escape the heat. Air conditioners perched on the roofs of most of the trailers.

Maybe Hedgepeth didn't live there, after all.

Flanked by dilapidated trailers on each side, Ben walked along in the dust as if looking for an address, but nobody stopped him or asked him why he was there. In Silverado, people probably didn't ask too many questions.

He reached the end of the park, turned the corner, going along the trailers parked in back by a rotting stake fence. Two cars were back there, one new, one old. A girl in a white blouse, short skirt, and high heels came out of an aluminum door, yelling "Forget it," and stamped over to the new car, got in, and raced away up the center lane, leaving exhaust and eukie smell.

Sweat was running off Ben's forehead and cheeks, down the valley of his chest, down the backs of his legs, part from heat and part from fear, something he'd learned a lot about during the last eight days.

Turning the corner of the outside row, the row that ran parallel to the road, he saw a white pickup. It was pulled in alongside the second trailer from the front end. He hadn't seen it when he walked into the park. It was diagonal to the swimming pool. Though he could only see one side, he knew it belonged to Thomas Hedgepeth. A Chevy; it was old.

Now all he had to do was check the license.

He hugged the right side of the lane, within arm's length of the line of trailers, having about four hundred feet to go.

Make sure of the license number, get to a phone, call Metcalf.

Without warning, when he was about two hundred feet away, the door to the second trailer from the end sprang open and there was Hedgepeth, in his blue tank top and khaki shorts, coming out with a cardboard box in his big hands.

Ben ducked back, sucking in the super-heated air, pulse pounding in his wrists, and then edged out again a moment later to take a second look.

Thomas Hedgepeth was hanging up laundry.

Not needing to see his license plate, Ben ran across the street, went between two trailers, and scrambled up the embankment, coming out on Los Coyotes about a hundred yards from the VW. Jilly's car had never looked better.

Running on up to where the bug was parked, puffing and panting when he reached it, he said to Sandy, "He's down there, all right. Go call Metcalf. I'm not about to use their phone." He'd seen a pay booth near the swimming pool.

"Why don't we both go?" Sandy said.

"I'll stay here in case he comes out, see which way he turns. Please, Sandy."

She didn't argue. Just nodded, meshed gears, pulled a U-turn on Los Coyotes, and headed for the pay phone at Soquel.

Surrounded

Sandy returned from Soquel, saying, nervously, "Deputy Metcalf is on his way. He wanted to know if you were sure that Hedgepeth is here."

"I'm sure," said Ben, trying to hide his own nervousness. He moved up by the hood of the VW.

About fifteen minutes later Metcalf arrived in his gray sedan, pulling up in front of Jilly's car, Sandy still inside it.

Another two unmarked cars pulled up behind it. Metcalf got out of the sedan and walked over.

"You think he's down there?"

Still standing by Jilly's hood, Ben said, "I know he's down there, Deputy. I saw him. He's in the second trailer from the front, on the right-hand side, across from the playground and pool. His truck is hidden by the trailer, so you can't see it from the entrance."

Metcalf nodded, saying, "I've called in a backup SWAT team from Santa Ana. They'll be here in about ten minutes.

I'm worried about his rifle. He might decide to hole up in there. Prefer that to prison."

Then Metcalf walked back to the other cars. In a moment, they went around the red VW, going up to the entrance and stopping, one car on either side, parking in opposite directions.

Sandy slid out, saying, "I hope no one gets hurt."

Metcalf came back to say, "You people stay here."

Then the gray sedan moved up near the entrance, and Metcalf got out again and went around to the trunk of his car. While Ben and Sandy watched, he removed a shotgun and loaded it; then removed his coat and put on a flak jacket.

Sandy said, "I'm not sure I want to see this."

Ben said, "He killed Rocky. He killed Rachel and The Sisters. He set that fire. He shot at me. He planned to kill my father. He may be insane, and I want him back in prison."

"I know all that. But I'd rather be a thousand miles from here right now. I don't even like to watch these things on TV."

Ben said, "I'll be glad to see this one handcuffed." He didn't want to talk any more about it and looked up the road to where Metcalf was. The deputy was leaning against the trunk of his car talking to a black officer who was also wearing a flak jacket and holding a shotgun.

On past the entrance about two hundred yards, a highway patrol unit had pulled across Los Coyotes, roof lights blinking, blocking the road. Ben looked in the opposite direction, behind them, and saw that another CHP car was blocking northbound traffic. He looked over at Sandy. She was biting her lip.

It was deadly still out there by the trailer park, no

breeze at all. So quiet. No traffic. The road shimmered. The whole place seemed ready to explode.

Then the SWAT van pulled up, coming from the north, and Metcalf walked over to talk to someone inside. Armed men got out of the two cars at the entrance, and then the van swung around, Metcalf and the black deputy walking beside it. Moving slowly, the van went down the incline to the Silverado Oaks entrance and stopped again.

Ben walked north until he could see down the embankment, through the eukie trees, to the first few trailers on the righthand side.

Hedgepeth's truck was still parked in the same position.

The door to his trailer was closed.

One of the SWAT team members, in his flak jacket and dark uniform, baggy pants tucked into boots, scooped the two children from the tire swing and ran down the road with them, one under each arm.

Other members of the team were spreading out around the trailer, taking up positions with automatic weapons.

Then Ben heard the loudspeaker that was mounted on the roof of the van: "Thomas Hedgepeth, this is Deputy Metcalf of the Orange County Sheriff's Department. You are completely surrounded. I order you to come out with your hands up. Leave any weapons that you have inside the trailer. I repeat—inside the trailer. We don't want to harm you."

Silence answered the deputy, and he repeated his words, adding, "We have twenty armed officers out here but want to avoid any use of weapons. I repeat, you are completely surrounded."

It seemed forever until the aluminum corrugated door

to the old trailer opened slowly, and then Thomas Hedgepeth stepped out into the shaft of sun hitting the wooden box that served as a step.

His hands were up and he was blinking.

He didn't look dangerous.

He looked frightened.

A Call from London

Thomas Hedgepeth's eyes lifted and linked with Ben's. They stared at each other briefly, the sniper finally looking away, looking back, then down. He seemed relieved it was over.

Ben still felt anger. Four animals were dead.

After Hedgepeth was led away in handcuffs, Sandy and Ben walked down into the park. Deputy Metcalf and several other officers were searching the trailer. Ribbons of yellow tape surrounded it, Police Line: DO NOT CROSS. Metcalf said it was okay to come inside.

About twenty-two feet long, up on cement blocks, it had dirty carpeting, worn down to bare plywood in some spots. Light fixtures were cracked or broken. The shower walls were coated with mildew. There was a musty, sweaty smell in there.

But what Ben mainly saw was a "Jepson" file spread everywhere: tabbed magazine articles about his dad and mother stacked on the yellow formica breakfast-nook table. He glanced at them. There were copies of newspaper clippings, in three separate folders, according to date, on the ripped pink naugahyde sofa. They began in 1973.

There were duplicates of his dad's scientific papers on a cracked maple lamp table in the so-called "living room."

Taped to the bathroom wall by the rusty medicine chest, half the mirror gone, was a large picture of Dr. Peter Jepson, eyes twinkling, smiling. Hedgepeth must have seen it every time he washed his face or brushed his teeth.

Sandy and Deputy Metcalf watched in silence as Ben looked at everything.

Ben felt ill, faint.

Then they went into the messy bedroom, and on the bed table were color photos of a beautiful little girl.

Chrissy Hedgepeth, Ben knew immediately.

They were very good pictures. Obviously, they were taken that day in the Halsey Zoo before Chrissy got entangled with the lioness who was guarding her cub. There she was, big smile on her face, petting the rabbits, goats, and mule deer.

Deputy Metcalf was in the doorway watching Ben.

Sandy went out first, dabbing at her eyes.

Then Ben went out, the bright smile on Chrissy's face going with him.

Metcalf said, "You can come down this afternoon to press charges on assault with a deadly weapon. Or in the morning, however you want."

Ben didn't answer.

"You can also charge him with assault on the animals."

Ben didn't answer.

Metcalf went on. "He'll be facing counts on theft of government property, on arson, and the Virginia authorities will get him for parole violation. He'll be in prison for a very long time, Ben."

Ben finally answered, feeling sorry, at last, for Thomas Hedgepeth. "I don't want to press any charges, Deputy. It's all over." He didn't think his dad would want to press charges either.

He took Sandy's hand, and they walked away from the stifling, smelly trailer into the brilliant sunlight.

Just after 4:00 A.M. the next morning, about the time that the sniper usually struck, the phone on the breakfast bar jangled, and Ben struggled out of bed.

Then he heard the familiar voice of the indestructible Dorothy Courtney-Jepson. Before he could ask "Are you okay? Where are you? Is Dad okay?" or even feel relief at her call, she was saying, "Child, we've got about three minutes to make the jet to London. Your father's buying the tickets now."

Ben demanded, "Where are you?"

"Nairobi."

"You're safe?"

"Yes, we're safe, but wait'll we tell what happened to us. It was wild. We'll call you from London. We'll be at the St. James. Are you all right?"

Ben said, "Yeah, yeah, I'm all right."

"We'll call from London, I promise. We want to see *Phantom of the Opera*. I have to go."

Ben raised his voice to a shout. He yelled across two continents and an ocean, "Mother, listen to me, dammit. *I kept it in the road*. Tell my dad!"

"I'm glad," she said. "Bye now."

There was a click from Nairobi.

He sat there a while, feeling great relief that they were safe but slowly understanding that not much had changed where she was concerned. Whatever "wild" had happened to them would turn into a book while Ben's story would be interesting but not all that significant, except to his dad, Alfredo, Sandy, Jilly, and himself. He decided that would be enough.

Sleep wouldn't be easy now, so he went back into his room, took the Palmer from the corner, went out to the redwood patio, and flopped down on the chaise lounge, nude as the day he was born. Most of the fierce heat still lingered in the canyon, and it must have been seventy-five degrees or more.

The animals were quiet. Maybe in their own way they knew the danger was over.

He began to softly three-chord:

Mammas don't let your babies grow up to be cowboys . . .

Don't let 'em pick guitars and drive an old bus; let 'em be doctors and lawyers and such . . .

When he'd finished the piece, he put the Palmer down, cupped his hands behind his head, and looked up at the stars. They were beginning to dim, seemingly pushed deeper into the sky by the coming of day.

So it was the Hotel St. James and *Phantom of the Opera*.

Ben thought about some of the things that had happened down here in the preserve while *they* were gone; since that first morning when the peacocks screamed.

Funny how the mind works: He might never be as tall

as she was, but he thought he could finally go eye-to-eye
with her. He was no longer mediocre, he knew. He'd never
been that way, he decided. And he thought he could finally
accept her the way she was.

When the first signs of gray-yellow dawn came up over
the San Bernardinos to the east, Ben went inside and got
dressed, slipping Willie Nelson and "Stay Away from
Lonely Places" into the boom box.

As old Willie sang, Ben reminded himself to hint to
Alfredo, once he left the hospital and was back on his feet,
that a new Zacatecas straw was needed.

Outside, Ben took a lead off the patio rail and went
straight to Number Fourteen, wondering if Nimbus would
come to the fence. The lion was awake, Ben saw, and trotted
over, a happy look on his young face.

As the lion moved toward the gate, Ben unlocked it,
tossing the chain around the big neck, saying, "We're going
for a walk, Nimbus."

And off they went down to the little path by the
Naranja, good friends already.